CRIMSON MOON

A Brown Angel Mystery

CRIMSON MOON

A Brown Angel Mystery

By

LUCHA CORPI

Arte Público Press
Houston, Texas

This volume is made possible through grants from the City of Houston through The Cultural Arts Council of Houston, Harris County.

Recovering the past, creating the future

Arte Público Press
University of Houston
452 Cullen Performance Hall
Houston, Texas 77204-2004

Cover design and art by Giovanni Mora

Corpi, Lucha, 1945–.
   Crimson Moon: A Brown Angel Mystery / by Lucha Corpi.
     p. cm.
   ISBN 1-55885-421-5 (pbk. : alk. paper)
   1. Private investigators—California—Fiction. 2. Mexican
American women—Fiction. 3. Civil rights movements—Fiction.
4. Mexican Americans—Fiction. 5. California—Fiction. I. Title.
PS3553.O693C75 2004
813'.54—dc21   2004041081
                                                   CIP

♾ The paper used in this publication meets the requirements of the American National Standard for Information Sciences—Permanence of Paper for Printed Library Materials, ANSI Z39.48-1984.

4 5 6 7 8 9 0 1 2 3   10 9 8 7 6 5 4 3 2 1

*To Manuel Ramos, Florence Hernández-Ramos
and Mark Greenside*

Acknowledgments

Mil gracias to fellow mystery writer Manuel Ramos and his lovely and accomplished wife Florence Hernández-Ramos for hosting my husband and me in Denver while I did research on the Crusade for Justice there. Their love for the city was contagious and their many contacts were extremely helpful. I am particularly grateful to Manuel for allowing Luis Móntez to serve as contact for Dora Saldaña during her investigation in the Mile-High city.

Also in Denver, I wish to thank Professor Luis Torres, artist Danny Salazar and his wife Maruca, Verónica Benavidez, Darold Vigil, and Rudy García for sharing their memories and knowledge with me, and Nita Gonzales for letting me visit with her at la Escuela Tlatelolco, one of the few Chicano institutions that has survived and continues to thrive since the time of the Chicano civil rights movement. Toni Fresquez, co-owner of Palabras con Sabor Coffeehouse and Bookstore and the *El Semanario* newspaper has my undying gratitude for letting me use her fabulous establishment in Denver as the setting for this novel.

In Oakland, I wish to thank Mark Greenside, who, through the years, has always taken the time to read and critique each of my first drafts, and given me invaluable suggestions. There are truly no words to express my immense gratitude to my husband Carlos Gonzales, who makes sure research photos are taken and catalogued and keeps me going with plenty of care, coffee, and nourishment during my long writing sessions.

As always, at Arte Público Press, my immense gratitude to my editors Nicolás Kanellos and Gabriela Baeza Ventura for not letting me get away with *literary murder*, and to Mónica M. Parle and Marina Tristán for their indefatigable efforts on behalf of my work and authorship.

Note: I have said it before, writing a novel can be compared to being married with children. It is a long-term commitment, and then, there are all these characters running around in my head, waking me up at odd hours, losing people, misplacing weapons, staining their clothes, putting themselves in harm's way, driving like crazy and driving me crazy. All in a mystery writer's workday. And all to say, writing a novel is a long process—four years, for me—and many changes take place during that time. So I report that the hand car wash in Denver has become a *Centro Humanitario para los Trabajadores*. The center provides a safe harbor for day laborers and assures that their rights are protected. Palabras con Sabor Coffeehouse and Bookstore has moved from its location on 22nd Street to richer coffee grounds in the affluent Cherry Creek area of Denver. The old Montgomery Ward site in Oakland was demolished and a brand-new elementary school now stands in its place. Day laborers in Oakland still gather six days a week around the Goodwill Industries site across from the school. Jerry Brown is still mayor of Oakland, but not for long. Thank goodness for change.

LC

Regret: The Last Cigarette

RAMONA SERNA did as she had been told. She lowered the window on the passenger's side, then stepped out of her car and closed the door with her hip. She rummaged through her fanny pack and took out a pack of cigarettes and a lighter. With both items in hand, she walked to the rail at Vista Point in the Oakland hills.

She leaned on the rail just enough to catch a glimpse of a small black oak tree growing precariously out of a thin brow about twenty feet below. A handful of leaves stuck to its twisted dried-up limbs. Two of its roots protruded from the ground; they stretched up like the arms of a child penitent asking heaven for mercy. The oak was either dead or dying, she thought. She shivered slightly as her bare knees touched the metal bars while her eyes moved quickly down then back up the fairly steep drop.

Her courage, she reflected, was made of brief moments like that one: Feet on the very edge, a glance thrown down a precipice then retrieved just in time to feel the tingle of the thrill but not the terrifying pull of her acrophobia. Her whole life had consisted of a series of such encounters with fear, of small and big triumphs over grief, guilt, sin, and a few others of death's tempting motivators.

After counting the cigarettes in the pack, she took one out. "Thirteen left," she whispered as she lit it. This was her countdown to smoking cessation. Lately, she had been misplacing items, finding it hard to remember where she had put important documents and old manuscripts, groping for familiar words. She had convinced herself that her recent memory lapses had to do with too much nicotine in her brain.

She inhaled once, deeply. She hadn't smoked since noon and blood rushed out of her brain with the first drag. Her eyeballs pulsated, her ears buzzed, and her thoughts briefly hovered in mid-mind unable to connect with others.

"There'll be none soon, no more nicotine highs, no more reasons for people to leave me alone if only for a short while," she said under her breath. Smoking had been so much a part of her life. A cigarette was a faithful companion, a priest sworn not to reveal the secrets she carried deep in her soul, available twenty-four hours a day to listen to her problems and sorrows, as old and loyal a friend as had been Elizabeth Ortiz-Saucedo, an attorney for the Port Authority, on whose behalf Ramona had come to Vista Point at sunset.

Elizabeth had asked her to call a number in Oakland and do as told. A throaty, slightly accented voice, perhaps that of a man, had given her instructions:

"Lower your passenger window. Walk to the rail at the far side of the parking area. Stand with your back to the car. A sealed large envelope will be left on your backseat. Do not look at the messenger. Wait ten minutes. Then deliver the package to the person whose name and address are written on it."

A scene worthy of a cheap spy novel or movie. She could come up with a better scenario than that one. She smiled. Imagined experiences were always more exciting than what people chose to call real life. But this was real life. And the events involved her best friend. She took another drag, letting the smoke in her lungs rob her brain of oxygen, allowing her not to focus on anything terribly real or serious. She looked briefly at her watch. It was five past seven. The messenger was supposed to arrive in a few minutes. She could use a large dose of brandy just about then. But she was trying to give up each and every one of her bad habits—her *vicios,* as her mother called them. *Vicios y madres.* Her mother. Better steer away from those memories.

Ramona smoked her cigarette and let her eyes wander from the twinkling lights of shuttles full of weary passengers landing at the Oakland airport on her left, past the tall cranes unloading containers at the Port of Oakland, across the water to the City by the Bay in her suit of lights, joined respectively to the East Bay and North Bay by the Oakland-San Francisco Bay Bridge and the Golden Gate Bridge. Her eyes followed the stream of lights on 101 North, then focused on the

San Raphael Bridge looping back to Richmond, then to Berkeley, completing the circle in Oakland.

Originally from Zacatecas, Mexico, Ramona's family had immigrated first to Los Angeles, then to Gilroy, California—"The Garlic Capital of the World"—where they had opened a very successful country store. But Ramona had called Oakland home since her graduation from U.C. Berkeley.

Elizabeth Ortiz-Saucedo, on the other hand, was an Oaklander by birth and had lived in Oakland even while she attended U.C. Berkeley and later Boalt Hall School of Law. She and Ramona had met at the Berkeley campus library, where they both worked part-time in the late sixties. Upon arrival in Berkeley, they had both been told that the campus community was the cradle of extremely liberal movements, which included the Free Speech and Anti-Vietnam War movements. Berkeley was the "Center of the Universe." Others differed, claiming that all "freedom" roads led to San Francisco, a charming arts mecca, home to the Beat and the Flower Power generations.

Oakland, however, was considered odd and unattractive by people living in "radical" Berkeley or "charming" San Francisco, to whom the mere mention of two words, "East Oakland," created fearful images of gun-toting Black Panthers, burly Hell's Angels on sleek wheels, African-American and Latino gangs raping women on every corner, and daily drug-related drive-by shootings.

To sports fans all over the Bay Area, Oakland was the home of the Athletics and the Raiders. The Coliseum was the only place they would visit a few times during the year, always careful to roll up their car windows as they traversed the "crime-ridden avenues" of East Oakland.

Oakland itself was home to people of countries from every continent. It sported all the skin colors of humanity. Its streets buzzed with words spoken in tongues never heard before, even by the most prescient charismatic prayer leaders. It was a unique city where the true metal of the American Dream was tested every hour of every day. Its inhabitants, at the end of the second millennium, looked upon Jerry Brown, a former California governor and now mayor of Oakland, to bring economic prosperity and justice to one of the most ethnically integrated communities in the United States.

With rekindled political fervor now, Elizabeth Ortiz-Saucedo hoped to run for the city council in the next election. Ramona had every intention of aiding her friend's cause. From the sketchy details supplied to her, Ramona surmised that the contents of the envelope were of a sensitive nature. Could they ruin Elizabeth's political aspirations? Is that why her friend had to avoid direct contact with either the messenger or the final recipient of the information?

Deep inside, she knew there was more to Elizabeth's request, something personal that required prudent handling of the package the messenger was about to deliver: Elizabeth's secrets, no doubt, what she had tried to keep from public scrutiny all these years. One secret bound her and Elizabeth together. But NO. She wasn't going to wade neck-deep through murky, treacherous waters.

Ramona heard a car pull up to the parking area behind her. An old if well-maintained VW beetle, she thought. The rather loud hum of the engine even when idling was unmistakable. The crunching of the gravel told of feet wearing hard shoes or boots and steps determined to span the distance between the two cars as quickly as possible.

She looked down but turned her head to the left just enough to glimpse the messenger as he approached her car. She caught sight only of his dark pants and boots. Unable to make out the color of the pants in the dimming light of sunset, her attention shifted quickly to his light-dark two-tone boots. A sniffle, a clearing of the throat, quick retreating footfalls, and the loud revving of the VW engine down the hill were all indicators that the presence intruding in the peaceful, red darkness of that mid-April's twilight was gone.

Having to wait another ten minutes before she could drive away, she took out another cigarette and lit it. This time, her vision remained unaltered. Her eyes focused on Venus high over the horizon and a few other celestial lights growing stronger as the day grew weaker.

Out of the corner of her eye, she caught a glimpse of the moon behind her. She turned and looked at it. Only half of the moon sphere was visible above the tree line at the top of the hill. The red twilight reflected on the thin veil of clouds covering the sphere, coloring it light crimson.

She turned her attention again to Oakland down below, then to the crimson sky. How perfect the moment, this ineffable, impeccable harmony between human and divine creations. Words, her daily staple, could never fully describe the perfection, and she sighed at the feeling of inadequacy such thoughts always left in their course through her mind.

She heard a rustling noise behind her and quickly turned. No one but the nearly full crimson moon was there, a silent conspirator in human affairs since the beginning of time. A car drove by and disappeared around a bend on the road ahead. Another car followed the first and began to slow down as it approached the parking area.

"Time to go," she said under her breath. Finishing her cigarette, she put out the smoking butt with her shoe. She unzipped her fanny pack and retrieved her car keys. The zipper got stuck. She slipped a finger under the zipper to loosen up the fabric caught in it. She could not. Frustrated, she pulled hard on it. The keys flew out of her hand. Without thinking, she lunged forward to grab them before they went over the rail. She managed to catch them in midair but tripped on the metal bars. She could have sworn that she had regained her balance, but an instant later she was going over the rail. An eclipsed crimson moon seemed to be the only witness. Her heart trembled. As if a huge bird had taken sudden flight inside her, something in her belly fluttered painfully. Things, people, and feelings she had not often allowed herself to experience whirled just inside skin and bone in her occipital lobe. The story she was writing left unfinished; the literary laurels she had hoped to garner; the men who abused her, then abandoned her; the mother who never came to visit; the daughter she could have had, but in reality could not.

Regret. In this, what she thought her last moment, all she could feel was overwhelming regret. This could not be her life. It was a borrowed life, something her imagination had invented. Had she also imagined that pressure on her back?

The protruding roots of the dying black oak broke her fall. The darkness beneath her eyelids happened so suddenly as to give her hardly a chance to further separate reality from imagination.

A car sped up the road. She could no longer hear it.

ONE
Prelude to Destiny

NINE O'CLOCK IN THE EVENING. The messenger had not shown up with the package Justin Escobar expected. He called the emergency phone number his client had given him. He did not recognize the woman's voice on the outgoing recording. Not that it mattered at that point whose voice it was. He had expected a person to answer the phone and explain the delay. He hung up without leaving a message.

His client, Elizabeth Ortiz-Saucedo, had stressed the need for immediate intervention and complete secrecy in dealing with the matter in his care. The need for concealment would become obvious to him as soon as he received the package with instructions, photos, and his retainer, she had told him. A friend of Elizabeth's would pick up the package at an undisclosed location and deliver it to him sometime between seven and eight in the evening.

There was only one problem. He had no idea what the business at hand was. He had agreed to handle this investigation only because Elizabeth had asked him.

He smiled. Elizabeth definitely had a flair for drama. He had not known anyone as versatile as she, yet so firmly devoted to her family and friends and the causes she embraced. She was smart and politically savvy, and she had a disarming smile and lots of *ángel*—charisma and extraordinary good luck. She also had a large group of very loyal friends, among them, their poet friends Art Bello and Myra Miranda, and, probably, the person in charge of the package Justin was to receive.

A week before, Justin had been surprised to get an invitation to a

1

reception at the Saucedos' home in the affluent district of Montclair. There, he was introduced to California Democratic senators and assemblymen, and other state and Oakland officials. He also met Elizabeth's second husband, Gastón Saucedo, a successful restaurateur and nightclub owner in the East Bay. Gastón was eleven years older than his wife. He had legally adopted her two daughters, Irene Ortiz and Serena Robles.

At the end of the reception, a visibly shaken Elizabeth had asked him to look into a "very delicate matter" for her. She would be in touch with him later on to let him know the details. He agreed.

What could that delicate matter be, he wondered as he waited for the messenger to arrive with the package. Blackmail? There had been many men in Elizabeth's life. The list included him. He and Elizabeth had had an intermittent year-long affair while they were students at Berkeley.

Without revealing names, Elizabeth had been open about her life, disarming any curious inquirers with a "Make no mistake, I am notorious, a woman with an *ethnically diverse* past—a true *Daughter of Oakland*." But she claimed to have been faithful to both her husbands, Ygnacio Robles and Gastón Saucedo.

The press found her style and candid attitude amusing and refreshing. Local media called on her whenever they needed a consultant on political issues of concern to Latinos in the Bay Area.

Art Bello, a mutual friend, had told Justin that Saucedo was very accepting of Elizabeth's romantic liaisons predating their five-year-long marriage. So for the time being Justin set aside the possibility that someone was blackmailing her. Still, not all the men in her life were accounted for. She herself had told him she hated only one man from her past, her daughter Irene's father. She had confessed that much to Justin that first autumn night in 1974, when she had come knocking on his door at midnight, distraught and shivering. But she never mentioned Irene's father's name.

Elizabeth. When they met, he found her intriguing, but he had no intention of getting involved with Liz Ortiz, a single mother with a young daughter. Liz was five years older than he and known to use up and throw away every lover she had ever had. That cold, moonless autumn night in 1974, however, the woman standing on his doorstep seemed so vulnerable he had to open his arms to her. They had sex that night and many others, always unplanned, always followed by walks on the long pier at the Berkeley Marina in the early morning, and breakfast at the Cafe Mediterranean on Telegraph Avenue. Then, they had each gone about their daily lives. About the time Justin graduated from Berkeley and Elizabeth got her law degree, she stopped knocking at his door in the middle of the night. He joined the police academy and moved to San Jose, where he got a job as a city cop.

Elizabeth married Ygnacio Robles, a building contractor. After the birth of her second daughter, Serena, Elizabeth returned to her political life, promoting Latino arts in the greater Bay Area, fund-raising to bring Chicano poets, musicians, and artists into the public schools, and working with the Fruitvale District Renovation Project in Oakland. Seven years later, amid rumors that Ygnacio Robles would be indicted for bribing city building inspectors to approve structures that were not up to code, he was found dead by his own hand in a motel room on Lombard Street in San Francisco. Elizabeth salvaged what she could of her husband's construction business and then went to work as an attorney for the Port Authority.

On a Friday evening, months after the funeral and after having sold her husband's construction company, Elizabeth unexpectedly showed up at Justin's door with a bottle of champagne.

The next morning, having slept little but still feeling restless, he suggested a very early breakfast at an all-night diner by the airport. But she declined. Instead, she cooked breakfast for them. After they ate and showered, Elizabeth got into her BMW and drove away and out of his life. A few months later, he read in the *Tribune* that she was about to marry Gastón Saucedo.

What, if anything, did all that have to do with Elizabeth's need for his services now? He would have to wait to find out.

He reached for the phone to call Gloria Damasco, his business partner, lover and companion for the past ten years. He changed his mind when he remembered that Gloria was meeting with Dora Saldaña, another private investigator. Dora and Gloria had reluctantly

TWO
Ghosts and Writers

DORA SALDAÑA LIKED TO BE IN THE COMPANY of strangers more than of friends. No doubt about it, she was a loner. Maybe that was partly the reason she had chosen to become a private investigator, she thought as she entered Heinold's First and Last Chance Saloon in Jack London Square. She liked the rugged, gold-rush era atmosphere of that hole-in-the-wall bar. There, the writer Jack London, his friends, and thousands of other seafarers and gold diggers had literally had their arrival or departure mug of ale, shot of whiskey, or some other favored firewater.

Dora ordered a margarita while she waited for her friend Gloria Damasco. Justin and Gloria had recently asked her to join their Brown Angel Security and Investigations Agency. Perhaps she would. She had a great deal of respect for Justin Escobar, and Gloria too had won her affection and admiration.

Gloria reminded Dora of her late father, Chuck Saldaña, a career U.S. Navy officer. Like her father, Gloria was able to straddle individualism and fellowship more successfully than most people. Dora hated to admit it, but she was more like her mother, Louisa, a highly individualistic woman, self-sufficient to a fault. How unfair it must have seemed to her mother to have a daughter who was so like her in spirit, yet much more outspoken, larger in size, and more physically active than she. A woman had to be self-contained and proper, able to survive anything life dished out, but also to show grace under pressure at all times. Dora could not help but admire her mother's courage.

A Navy family was like a tumbleweed, on the move more often

than not. She and her family had lived in the Philippines, Panama, Texas, South Carolina, Hawaii, and finally California. Looking back, her mother had fared well in that kind of life, precisely because she could function without much assistance from anyone. Being so able to take care of herself and her children during her husband's long absences, her mother had come to believe that she really needed no one.

After their father's death, Dora and her brothers chose to stay in the San Francisco Bay Area and attend college there. Louisa moved to a small town in the Sierra Nevada, near Lake Tahoe, where she could be by herself, away from any mundane cares.

By the time Louisa died, her only friends were the owners of a small general store where she shopped once a week. The storekeepers suspected that something was wrong when Louisa failed to pick up her groceries two weeks in a row. Concerned, they called on her only to find her sprawled on the kitchen floor, frozen to death. The sheriff told Dora that Louisa had fallen and fractured her hip and leg. When she tried to move, the broken leg bone had ripped an artery, causing a hemorrhage. The cell phone Dora had given her mother, and for which she had obviously paid a useless monthly service fee, was on Louisa's night table still wrapped in Christmas tissue.

Her mother's need for solitude and her self-sufficiency had become a trap. That thought always led Dora to questions for which she would never find comforting answers. Why had she not paid more attention to her mother's emotional needs? Why had she not been aware of her mother's fragile mental state?

Dora went about her days skittering over her emotional quagmires. But the evening before her meeting with Gloria, when Beatrice Constantino, her client, came to her door, Dora saw in her the same pained look she observed in her mother's eyes whenever she had to ask for anyone's help. She knew she was going to have a hard time refusing Beatrice's request, whatever it was.

"Can I get you another one, Hon?" the bartender at The First and Last Chance Saloon asked, interrupting Dora's mental soliloquy.

"Sure," she replied.

When she saw Gloria Damasco walk in, she told the bartender, "And one for my friend here." Turning to Gloria she asked, "What's up, partner?"

"Not much. Just trying to get some paperwork done before my mom and I leave for the mountains. She wanted to go to Reno, do a little gambling. But I didn't. We settled for Lake Tahoe's South Shore. Plenty of casinos there, too. She can wrestle with all those one-arm bandits, and I can catch up with my reading, rest, and go for walks around the lake."

The bartender came back with their drinks.

Gloria sipped hers. "What's going on with you?"

"I'm working a missing-person case. It involves a writer. Since you have a lot of contacts among the Latino literati, I thought you might be able to find out if any of them knows something about this missing writer. Also, as you'll see, this guy writes about the Third World Student Strike at U.C. Berkeley, back in the sixties. I know you participated in the strike, so you might be able to recognize the writing." Dora paused. "I have to warn you, though. If you agree to do this, it'll have to be pro bono. I'm not charging my client for my services either."

"I'm not sure how I can help in such a short time, but I'll try. *Gratis*. No problem," Gloria said, already intrigued. "So, are we talking about a novelist? *¿Hombre o mujer?*"

"You tell me," Dora answered, handing Gloria a folder with about sixty tattered lavender pages.

Gloria skimmed through the text, stopping to read short passages from time to time. "Damn right, it's about the strike, but I have no idea who might have written it. Where'd you get it?"

"Beatrice, my client, gave it to me," Dora said. She was pensive for a while, then asked, "Could this be autobiographical? Man or woman?"

"This narrative is in first person, but that doesn't necessarily mean that it's autobiographical. Man or woman—I couldn't say for sure, except that the lavender paper's not exactly a guy's choice. Do you suspect your client wrote it? But why would she . . . I don't understand."

"I already asked her. Beatrice told me she didn't write it."

"So what's with her? And where did she find this manuscript, anyway?" Gloria asked, looking closely at the papers. "Trivial as this may sound, these are coffee stains. Those look like strawberry jam. I don't dare venture a guess about those brown smears on page one."

"She found it at the municipal dump, on Wednesdays, over several weeks, to be more specific. A chapter here, second installment the week after, and so on."

"That's weird. What was your client doing at the dump?"

"Beats me. Beatrice was a homeless person for many years. That is until Sharon, my landlady, met her in a shelter some years ago. Beatrice does odd jobs for me from time to time, but she's really Sharon's housekeeper. Beatrice hardly charges me for her services. Partly, that's why I accepted to look into this for her. At any rate, in a nutshell, she's a chronic depressive. In her late teens, she attempted suicide. Her parents couldn't handle her and they had her committed. She ran away from Highland Hospital's psych ward and disappeared for several months. The police caught up with her and brought her back home. Her mental condition deteriorated and she tried to kill herself again. She ended up at Highland's psych ward again. But this second time, a new psychiatrist there diagnosed her as a depressive, put her on the right medication, and literally saved her life. Beatrice told me he also introduced her to literature. But Mom and Dad, however, afraid of what she might do if she had a relapse, didn't want her living with them. She eventually ended up on the streets, unable to hold a job, scavenging for bottles and cans to sell just to eat.

"Sometimes, she would spend the night at a shelter where Sharon, my landlady, was a volunteer. Sharon told me that one rainy afternoon, she saw Beatrice reading a book, *Anna Karenina*, which Sharon had read. Sharon got curious and struck up a conversation with Beatrice about the novel. She was impressed. Beatrice was definitely an unusual person, and Sharon took pity on her. Eventually, Sharon offered Beatrice room and board and some cash in exchange for housework, cooking, and gardening. Sharon also pays for Beatrice's medical expenses."

Dora sipped her margarita, then continued, "I don't exactly know why Beatrice keeps going back to the dump, even now. Regardless, as long as she takes her medication, she's functional, though she tends to take things too much to heart," Dora chuckled. "Take her scrapbook. She recently showed it to me. She has this theory that any Mexican-American singer who's on the brink of making it in the Anglo music world has been or will be a victim of a violent death. She cites as examples Richie Valens and Selena."

"Hmmm. Hadn't thought about that."

"Anyway, as you can see, she's on a different wavelength, and pretty obsessive, like with finding this writer. She's convinced that this guy's in danger."

Gloria was quiet for a while, then said, "Tell me something. If she found these excerpts at different times, how did she know where to look for them?"

"Ah, the million-dollar question. Well, she told me that she usually looked in the recycling area of the dump. The second time, she wrote down the number of the truck that dumped the stuff. No. 649-OK. The week after, she followed that truck and found the third manuscript installment. And so on." Anticipating Gloria's question, she added, "649-OK services the Laurel District in Oakland, the area between High Street and 35th Avenue and MacArthur Boulevard and Mountain Boulevard. Any suggestions?"

Gloria frowned and shook her head. She gave Dora an inquisitive look.

"What?"

"I'm just wondering why you agreed to do this. I mean, so much effort on behalf of a client who's not paying you, and of a writer, who, for all you know, might have just voluntarily gone someplace else to write." Gloria looked Dora in the eyes. "C'mon. Give. There's more to it, isn't there?"

"Not what you think." Dora took a sip of her margarita. "I don't know how to explain it. I wish I could just say no to Beatrice, but I can't." She threw her head back and sighed. "I've told you about my mother and me. No matter how much she rejected me, or rather, how much she preferred my brothers' company to mine, I still can't shake this feeling off that I didn't do anything for her when she needed my help most. Maybe this is difficult for you to understand. You have such a good relationship with your mother and daughter. I want to believe my mother loved me. But it was obvious she didn't like me, she didn't approve of me. Still, I should have gone to see her more often, to be there to help her, even when she didn't want me there."

"You were the child, not the mother in the relationship. You have to stop blaming yourself," Gloria offered.

Dora wiped a bit of moisture from her eyes with the back of her index fingers, then said, "Beatrice reminds me so much of my mother. It pains her so to ask for something, anything. It must have been very tough for her to come to me, even for such a small favor as this. How can I say no to her?" She paused. "Besides," she chirped, "how difficult can it be to find a writer?"

"Just hard enough to keep your skills honed," Gloria said, and patted Dora's hand to comfort her. "Well, I'd suggest you start with Poets & Writers, an organization in New York. They have a national directory. It lists only published writers. But you could look at their California listing and see if any of the writers in Oakland live in the Laurel District. In the meantime, I'll contact Art Bello and Myra Miranda, both poets, both participants in the Third World Student Strike at Berkeley. Remember them? They were at Justin's birthday party last year."

"Sure do."

"My mom and I are leaving tomorrow afternoon. I'll drop off a copy of the manuscript for them to look at tomorrow morning." Gloria scribbled both poets' phone numbers on the manuscript and handed it back to Dora.

"Shoot! I almost forgot. There's a phone number on the back of a page . . ." Dora leafed through the manuscript, turning a page over to show Gloria.

"Area code 303."

"Denver, Colorado. I called the number last night. I got an answering machine and left a message. Nothing so far. I'll call the number again as soon as I get home. I'm dying to see if my new tracer works. You know how unreliable caller-ID devices are, so I got this little gadget online that hooks up to my computer. This guy calls and bingo! I'll have his name and address."

"Sounds like a useful little toy. Maybe Justin and I will get one for the office, too. By the way, have you given any more thought to becoming the third partner at Brown Angel?"

"Still thinking about it. I'll tell you when you get back from South Shore. I promise."

"Good enough." Gloria drained her glass. She pulled her address book and a small memo pad out of her handbag. She looked for a name in it and scribbled the information down. "Listen, if your tracer fails, give this guy in Denver a call. Luis Móntez. He's an attorney there. Justin met him last year. He speaks highly of Móntez. You never know. You might need his help." She put the slip of paper on the table. "Why don't we go and make a copy of this manuscript?" She got up.

"Ahead of you already," Dora said, handing Gloria a couple of copies.

They split the tab. Gloria said good-bye at the door and Dora walked across Jack London Square towards Embarcadero Street. An Amtrak was pulling into the Oakland train station, blocking her way across Embarcadero. Three short whistles alerted everyone to another train ready to roll as soon as the Amtrak left the station. She had once calculated that about thirty trains passed through Oakland to and from the Port on any given day. Like a foghorn in the mist, a train whistle in the distance never failed to arouse in her an inexplicable longing for a journey to some familiar, yet unknown place. But this was not the time to be thinking about journeys. It was time to head home to a distant stranger.

THREE
No Sanctuary from Violence

ELIZABETH ORTIZ-SAUCEDO waited for Justin Escobar at the entrance to the county's Highland Hospital trauma center.

An hour earlier, the police had phoned to tell her that her friend Ramona had apparently been the victim of an accident at Vista Point. A jogger passing by her car had become suspicious, looked over the ravine, and spotted Ramona unconscious twenty feet below.

Elizabeth had to wait until the physician in charge of her friend's case could talk to her. She looked around for an empty seat, but the waiting area was packed with a throng of humanity clutching various parts of their anatomy, crying, moaning. Some sat alone, others were accompanied by their children or parents. It was ten in the evening, Thursday, April 13, 2000. Where had life gone?

Elizabeth decided to stand in a corner, away from the main waiting area. From that vantage point, she could still keep an eye on both the curtained entrance to the ward and the parking lot. She realized there was no sanctuary from violence and suffering anywhere there, as she watched in horror as a tall, hefty, young man repeatedly hit an older man lying on a gurney. The older man showed a large, bleeding arm gash. Paramedics and cops rushed to restrain the young man. He furiously resisted being handcuffed. Taking two paramedics down with him, he crashed on another empty gurney, a few feet from where Elizabeth stood.

Her breathing quickened and her hands began to shake. She wanted to take her eyes away from the scene, but she could not. All sorts of memories she had managed to bury underneath thirty years of living raged in, unexpectedly and uncontrollably. Her mind's eye filled again with the violent scene of highway patrolmen, sheriff's deputies, Berkeley and U.C. campus cops beating, gassing, handcuffing, dragging, kicking unarmed young Chicano, Black, Asian, and Native-American students.

Her mind had refused to forget one particular occasion, long ago. How could she forget? Her life had changed forever that day. She tried to brush the memory away, but her will to remember was stronger. Her hands automatically moved up, and she covered her face with them. As if it were happening at that moment, she felt again the pull of a hand dragging her away from the bloody confrontation, about the time a helmeted sheriff's deputy sprayed her with mace. She lunged at the deputy, but someone held her back. As she fought to free herself from the hand pulling her away from the cop, through the layer of gas and tears veiling her eyes, she saw her friend Ramona close by. Ramona was being clubbed and shoved against an unmarked police car. Another cop stepped on Elizabeth's hand, then struck her with his club, knocking her unconscious. Just before she passed out, she thought she heard someone close to her say, "Put her in the car. Move!"

The next day, she woke up in a bed at Highland's emergency ward. Every inch of her body ached. But her chest and mind were filled with rage. Ethnic rage. Impotent rage against an infamous, faceless enemy. Ramona Serna lay in another bed near hers, with a mild concussion, bruised rib cage, a black eye, and the saddest look Elizabeth had ever seen in anyone's eyes.

Thirty years after that episode, standing by the entrance to the hospital as she waited for Justin Escobar, Elizabeth regretted having asked her longtime friend Ramona to go to Vista Point and pick up that package for her. But Ramona had insisted on doing it. Against her better judgment, Elizabeth had agreed. Her daughter and granddaughter's future depended on their absolute discretion. She had to keep her affairs away from media scrutiny. Someone, in time, would get hold of the news, find out what she was up to, but she wanted to postpone that moment. To ward off anyone's interference with Justin's investigation, she had avoided personally handling any event connected with it. It was obviously too late for those concerns, she thought.

Elizabeth probed her conscience. As far as she and Gastón could project, there was no danger involved. After getting the package from the messenger, Ramona was to deliver it to Justin Escobar. Nothing was supposed to happen to Ramona. But something had happened to her. What, exactly?

Elizabeth swallowed hard to contain the tears threatening to gush out. She had to remain calm and collected. Everyone's safety depended on her ability to keep her wits about her. She was glad she had Gastón's unconditional support. She had never before known that love could be a magnanimous feeling. She had always considered love a surrogate for jealousy, mistrust, possessiveness, and pettiness. Before meeting her second husband, she had not understood that love was not evil but was just being used by evil people to hide their low and mean designs.

A long time ago, Justin had told her something similar. Justin. There was no regret when she thought about their love affair. From the moment they met at a MECHA student meeting on campus, she liked him. It was perhaps his nonjudgmental attitude that she liked most. She was certainly impressed with his intellect, and in awe of his ability to focus on a situation and put it in a proper frame of thought and action. But most of all, she admired his courage. Courage in the face of adversity. Courage to embrace a cause without thinking immediately what was in it for him. Courage to love his friends unconditionally.

Why had she stopped seeing him? She still remembered that October night in 1975 when she decided not to see him again. A very difficult decision she regretted for a long time afterwards, but one that she'd postponed making far too long at the time. She wasn't ready to make a long commitment to anyone. But life had other plans for her. A year later, despite her promise to herself not to get married, she accepted to marry Ygnacio Robles, knowing full well she wasn't in love with him. She rejected his proposal at first, but changed her mind when she realized that her daughter Irene, who was seven at the time and attended a parochial school, had become the subject of scorn by her young peers. For the first time, her little girl had asked why her father never came to visit her or take her to school. Irene already showed signs of depression. Ygnacio, who had won Irene's affection, was a perfect father for her daughter. Serena was born a few years later, and Irene was happy. Elizabeth was content. Then one day Ygnacio was found dead by his own hand. He was about to be indicted for bribing city officials and racketeering.

After his death, Irene had lost that father, too. She had blamed Elizabeth and accused her of driving Ygnacio to suicide. But how could Elizabeth explain to her young daughter that the painful choices she, as a mother, had to make were always with Irene's well-being in mind? How could she tell her child that at times men found death's prospects more appealing than a life of public shame and imprisonment?

Elizabeth wrestled with Ygnacio's decision to end his life, with her feelings of guilt for not seeing what was coming, for not having loved him enough. But her daughters' future and her own were at stake, so she concentrated on her late husband's construction business affairs, sold his company and went back to work, landing a good job as an attorney with the Port Authority.

She was not one to live with regret or fear for very long. She owned up to every mistake she'd made. She did her best for Irene, and later for Serena as well. In the end, with the help and support of her parents, she managed to land on her feet.

Someone up there, or wherever heaven was, liked her. But that was not the case with Ramona, who had a lifelong, strained relationship with her mother.

Angelina, "Lena," Serna was a moral tyrant who saw her daughter's past and present life as nothing less than evil. She disliked everything her daughter stood for. Ramona swore she did not care what her mother thought of her; as long as she had her writing, she could live with her mother's disapproval. But Lena's lack of love and support had always been at the center of Ramona's low self-esteem.

Elizabeth knew of no one more creative and hardworking than Ramona. But her friend's published work had attracted little recognition from either Latino or Anglo mainstream readers.

During a visit to Black Oak Books in Berkeley, years earlier, Ramona had asked Elizabeth, "You see those portraits of writers above the bookcases?" When Elizabeth nodded, Ramona added, "My photo will never be among them. These people will never consider me, or any other Chicano or Chicana writer, worthy of their company."

The sadness in Ramona's voice was compelling. And Elizabeth, who was quite busy at the time, offered to put her friend in touch with some people who could help her market her work more efficiently. Ramona could begin to write stories that were more appealing to a larger audience. She could get a high-powered agent or publicist to push her work and her authorship. Elizabeth even contacted some of those agents for her friend, but Ramona never followed up on those leads. About that time, her friend began to drink heavily. Ramona had experimented with mind-altering drugs back in college but never to the extent of losing touch with reality and not being able to function.

Elizabeth began to suspect that her friend was perhaps more afraid of success than failure. She well understood why, since no one knew Ramona's troubles better than she. Did her friend know now, lying on a gurney somewhere in the ER, how much Elizabeth had always cared for her? Did she realize that all it really took was to own up to your own mistakes openly and make up for the ones you could in order to beat life at its own game?

"Oh, God, please help her. What's done is done. At least I have Irene and Serena; Ramona has her poetry," she reminded herself. But it all was hopeless if Ramona remained in a coma as a result of her near-fatal fall at Vista Point.

The police had so far ruled her fall accidental. But was it? Had Ramona finally decided to end her life as she had threatened so many times before? Elizabeth prayed that it was really an accident. But how could she explain to the police that the large envelope, which was supposed to be in Justin's hands now, was missing? How could she possibly give the facts to the police without exposing her reasons for secrecy?

Elizabeth tried to contain her anxiety and grief, but the tears had begun to flow. She had neither the energy nor the desire to hold them back any longer. It actually felt good to cry, better than trying to ignore the oppressive feeling in her chest, or to hush an inner voice warning of imminent tragedy.

She was patting her eyes and nose dry with a tissue when she caught a glimpse of Justin walking across the parking lot. Personal emotions, she believed, should always be privately expressed. Gastón and Ramona had been the only people in this world she had allowed to peer into what she considered her weaknesses. Crying and public displays of anger topped that list. She truly believed that it was impossible to control what others did, but it was always possible to control what she did. For a woman with political ambitions, self-control meant the triumph of reason, particularly in the face of adversity. It was courage by any other name. And, in her book, courage was what separated mediocrity from greatness. She had the feeling she would need a large dose of valor in days to come.

Justin walked in and immediately asked, "What's going on?"

Elizabeth related the little she knew about Ramona's accident and mentioned that her friend was the person in charge of delivering an envelope to him. Gastón had made the arrangements. The envelope had been delivered to Vista Point, but it was not among Ramona's personal belongings now.

"Are you sure the envelope was already in her possession?"

"Yes. Gastón already looked into it. It was delivered exactly as instructed and within the time frame."

"I don't mean to question your husband's veracity. But I'd like to talk to the messenger myself, if I may. Just to make sure. What's his name and the name of the company he works for?" Justin took out a small memo pad and pen.

"Mensajero, on Lakeshore Avenue. I don't know the name of the messenger. But the owner, Mitch Quintana, is Gastón's *compadre*. My husband even lent him the money to start his business. They go back a long way. Gastón trusts Mitch implicitly."

"Would you mind asking Gastón to phone Mr. Quintana and inform him I'll be stopping by? It'll make it easier to get his help."

"*Pues, seguro.* I'll do it right away." Elizabeth took out her cell phone. After a brief conversation with her husband, she hung up.

"One more thing. Why did the cops contact you directly?" When Elizabeth gave him a puzzled look, Justin said, "I don't mean to grill you, but all details are important until we know how the pieces fit."

"Ramona carried a card in her wallet with my name as the person to contact in case of an emergency along with my number at home."

"Was my retainer a check or cash?"

"Cash."

"Do you think someone might have watched you put the money in the envelope, maybe followed you, then the messenger?" Justin asked.

"No one other than Gastón."

"Okay. What was in the envelope, besides the cash, and what did you expect me to do with that information? That is, if you still want me to look into it for you."

"In the envelope was a key that belonged to Irene's father. There was also a photo of a man who could be her father. It's an old photo. I'm sorry you have so little to go on, but I urgently need you to find him for me."

All sorts of painful feelings crisscrossed Justin's chest. For years, he had assumed that Elizabeth knew who Irene's father was. He looked at her. She met his glance but lowered her eyes immediately. She blushed. He felt embarrassed. Judgment was a right entirely reserved for her husband and children. His concern was to do what was right for her as his client.

Elizabeth, however, as if in answer to his unspoken question, added, "I know it sounds incredible that I wouldn't know for sure who Irene's father is. I'll just have to ask you to set that aside for now. It's urgent we find him soon. I think I told you Irene has a baby. Gabi, my granddaughter, is suffering from a rare form of bone marrow disease. She needs to have transfusions and a bone marrow transplant. All of us in the family have been tested, including Gastón and Irene, and other friends. But none makes a good donor. The odds of finding a match are staggering. My only hope rests on your finding Irene's father. He might still be alive, somewhere, maybe even has other kids who might be able to . . ."

Elizabeth's voice quavered. She ran her fingers through her long hair as if to brush away her despair. She reached into her briefcase and retrieved a large envelope for Justin. "I made a copy of both sides of the key and a computer-enlarged copy of his photograph and a few mug shots. As clear as the enlargement is, I don't know how helpful it may be in the end."

"We'll see." The prospects of finding a man who was at least thirty years older and a key without an address were as low as winning the power ball lottery.

Justin took out the contents and looked at the copies of the key. It looked like a regular Masterlock key, smaller than a door key. Perhaps the key to a closet or locker. Engraved on both sides were the numbers 776689 and the usual "Do Not Duplicate" warning.

The photo enlargement showed the face and torso of a medium-built man, who, judging by his facial features and hair, could be African American. The upper part of a U.S. mailbox was visible. Although he was leaning back on the mailbox, he towered over it a good eighteen inches. Possibly five-feet-nine, perhaps ten, Justin thought, but could not guess his age. In the style of the late sixties, the man wore an Afro hairdo with a thin red bandana tied behind his head, long sideburns, and a bit of curly fuzz on each side of his upper lip and on the hollow just below his lower lip.

Protruding from his right pocket, Justin could see a round key holder that looked like an Aztec calendar and a half chain hanging out of the man's right pants pocket. It looked like a candid shot, not at all posed. The man looked on a group of young people, possibly students, holding picket signs, marching outside a building unfamiliar to Justin.

"Where was this taken?"

"At the draft office in Oakland," Elizabeth answered.

More out of habit than curiosity, he flipped the photo over, and was surprised to see the man's personal data. "'OZ', William Ozuna, 1969."

"How long did you and Oz . . ." Justin paused, groping for the right words.

Smiling this time, Elizabeth said, "I met him in 1968, when he came to Berkeley. He wasn't a student at Cal, but he was a member of the Hayward Brown Berets. He was also a Korean War vet, charismatic and much older than the rest of us. He was always offering to teach Ramona and me how to shoot. Ramona went target shooting with him. I never did. Guns have always scared the hell out of me. But I can't say that I wasn't attracted to him. So was Ramona, and every other Chicana at the time. I don't exactly know why I had an . . . affair with him—if that's what you'd call a couple of brief encounters. I had been seeing Rudy Ballesteros and our relationship was going well . . . I was a mess, back then."

"Could Ballesteros be Irene's father and not this guy?"

"Rudy isn't Irene's father. Anyway, I was with Willie Oz only twice. I stopped seeing him partly because I didn't like his . . . bed manners. But I also found out that he had a wife, a *gabacha* by the name of Muriel, and two young children. They lived in Hayward."

"How did you find that out?"

"About two weeks after our second encounter, Art Bello saw Willie with his wife. Art had to park off campus and was walking to the Student Union to take part in an antidraft demonstration at Cal State Hayward. Willie and Mrs. Oz were sitting in a car, having a brown bag lunch. Art didn't like Willie to begin with, and seeing him so cozy with this Anglo woman made Art dislike him even more. Not because he was married to an Anglo, but because he had lied about his marriage to her." Elizabeth shook her head. "The things men did for *la Causa*—and women, too. You might remember that at the time 'two-hundred percent Chicanos' were in denial and abandoned their Anglo wives and offspring so as not to be called 'coconuts' by their brown brothers. Sad, isn't it? We spent so much time questioning each other's loyalty and ethnic credentials that we couldn't see the real enemy right under our noses. Oh, well. . . . No use going over what we did or should've done." She shrugged her shoulders.

"So what was the deal with him and his wife?"

"Art went up to the car and greeted Willie. Art told me that Willie's face turned every color of the rainbow. Mrs. Oz—Muriel Ozuna, as she introduced herself to Art—on the other hand, was delighted to meet one of Willie's friends. Art was furious when he also found out that Muriel Ozuna was working as a secretary at Cal State's Admissions to support the family while Willie was 'finishing his degree at Berkeley.' The man was a liar and a fake."

"Was he Black?" Justin asked.

"Nope. He was *puertorriqueño*, actually Nuyorican, born in New York of Puerto Rican parents. Or so he said, still trying to fit in. Didn't matter. After Art saw Oz and his wife, Willie kept his distance. He still came around and talked big about "The Revolution" and all that, but he stopped playing the role of lover boy."

"When was the last time you saw him?"

"In February of 1969, a few hours before the Blue Meanies— sorry, the sheriff's men—and the other cops showed up on campus. He told Ramona that he was going to get his gun because he knew this was going to be 'the fucking mother of all battles.' We were about to make history, and he was going to be ready for the pigs. He had his keys in his hand. He dropped the key ring. It must have come apart and one of the keys was left on the ground. He didn't notice and rushed out. I picked up the key and ran after him, but I couldn't catch up with him. Neither Ramona nor Art or I ever saw him again. Eventually, we thought he was just a 'wannabe.' Truth is, too much was going on, and no one, including me, missed Willie much. Of course, eight and a half months later I was taking Baby Irene home. I could not conceive of giving her away, just like that, like a pair of unwanted jeans you pass on to someone else."

Elizabeth lowered her gaze and stared at the floor for a while. When she looked at Justin again, a couple of tears hung precariously from her lashes. She blinked and the tears found a course down her cheeks. She patted her eyes dry with a tissue, then said, "I was happy to have a daughter, alive and well. My parents also loved her from the start. I've been blessed with wonderful parents and two beautiful daughters. That's all that's mattered to me for years, until a few months ago, when Irene had her own daughter." She blew air through her open mouth. "And now this. I never thought Ramona was going to get hurt. Thirty years ago, she trusted me and . . . and now . . . again . . ." Her voice broke.

What could he say that would be of any comfort to her. Nothing. The warmth of his arms was the only comfort he could offer her. He led her to an empty seat and went to get some water for her. Unable to find a drinking fountain in the immediate area, he got a canned soft drink for Elizabeth and a cup of coffee for himself from vending machines. As he walked back to the waiting area, he saw Elizabeth talking with a doctor.

"We'll know more in twenty-four hours," the ER physician was saying as Justin approached. "But, in cases like hers, it's very difficult to predict what's going to happen. Your friend might regain consciousness in the morning or it might take days, weeks. We simply can't tell. Not just yet."

"May I see her?" Elizabeth asked.

"She's being moved to ICU shortly. You're welcome to stay with her if you'd like. Check with ICU in a half hour or so. They'll tell you where your friend is. Good luck."

A half hour later, Justin walked Elizabeth to the elevator. She held on to his hand until the elevator door closed.

FOUR
Palabras con Sabor

DORA WALKED UP A BRICK PATH alongside the main house towards the in-law cottage she rented from Sharon. She chased the scent of roses and the sound of running water from the fountain in the courtyard to her door. She glanced at the rear windows of the main house. Her client Beatrice's room faced the courtyard. Her lights were out. Dora was grateful her client liked to go to bed early. Beatrice would probably be knocking at her door first thing the next morning.

She unlocked the door and stepped in. A Carmen Lomas Garza painting, hanging above a boxed "Ofrenda" by Patricia Rodríguez, greeted her. She put her keys and handbag on the table at the entrance, slid out of her shoes, and headed towards her office to check her computer and the tracer. She reviewed the instructions for the tracer. "Use the headphones. Press the red button on the third ring. Keep caller on line at least thirty seconds or tracer will not be activated. Phone and address will flash on separate windows. 15 seconds. To retrieve numbers and messages type in DoraTwo." She typed in her password. The tracer was working well, but there were no messages.

She had just walked into her bedroom to change when the phone rang. She rushed back to her office, put on the headphone, pressed the red button in it, and greeted the caller.

After a brief silence, a man's grave and accented voice said, "Joo call me. Wat joo wan?"

"Hmmm. A Spanish accent," Dora thought. To the caller, she said, "Thank you for returning my call, sir." Dora paused to force the man to talk.

"Who'r joo, wha'joo wan?"

Dora thought of switching to Spanish, but the man's inability to understand her might just keep him hooked long enough. She spoke deliberately and slowly. "I'm calling on behalf of Beatrice Conrad. She is the publisher of Midnight Books in Berkeley, California. We are a small press, but our books are carried by most major distributors on- and off-line. Ms. Conrad came across a copy of a partial manuscript by you. She'd like to know if you'd consider submitting the complete manuscript for consideration at Midnight Books. If you give me your address, I'll be happy to send you a copy of our standard contract." Dora paused when she heard the man at the other end snort.

"She said joo call me, no? She." The man sounded exasperated.

Hoping to keep him longer on the line, in a mellifluous tone she said, "Of course Ms. Conrad said to call you. She's very interested in your manuscript. Let me be frank with you. Ms. Conrad feels that you have a good story here. By the way, is it autobiographical? That would make it even more appealing."

The man was quiet for a few seconds, but he did not hang up. Dora knew his curiosity was piqued. She decided to wait and let him make the next move.

"No. She said call me," he repeated. "She wans talk me. She come here."

"She's very busy at the moment." Dora paused. When the man did not answer, afraid that she might lose him, she quickly added, "Ms. Conrad has edited and published many books. She's quite interested in publishing yours."

"Say her, she come here. No deal."

"It's a great deal. Believe me," Dora said.

"Book. No eenterestéd. Sank'u. She come. No deal," the man said and hung up before Dora had a chance to say another word.

"Gotcha!" She quickly jotted down the information on the screen. She read it aloud: "(303) 697-0055, Palabras con Sabor, Bookstore and Coffeehouse, 617 22nd Street, Denver, Colorado."

She waited a few minutes, then dialed the number in Denver.

"Palabras con Sabor," a woman answered.

"Sorry to bother you, but someone just called me from this number. He left this number but didn't leave his name. Could you look around and see if he's still there?" Dora asked the woman.

"You're probably talking about Jesse Latour. He just left. I'm sorry but we're now closed," the woman told Dora. "But would you like to leave a message? I know he doesn't have a phone. I think he's been expecting your call."

"Expecting my call. Hmm," Dora thought. To the woman, she said, "I'd rather talk with him directly. I'm assuming it's a pay phone I'm calling."

"No. It's the coffeehouse phone. We let our regulars use it. Jesse usually comes in around eleven every morning."

"Next time I'm in Denver, I'll be sure to look you up. Sounds like a great establishment you have there."

"We'll try our best to please you," the woman said and hung up.

Dora logged off and removed her headset. "Odd," she mumbled under her breath as she recalled what Jesse had said: *"She said call me. Say her, she come here. No deal."* The woman at Palabras con Sabor had mentioned that he was expecting a call from a woman, supposedly herself. Who was the woman Jesse Latour had referred to? Of course, that woman had to live in Oakland. Or maybe he had not realized he was calling Oakland. The area code would be enough for him to know, though. Still, it made no sense to return a long distance call if he did not know who was calling him. Why was this woman pursuing Latour?

It doesn't matter, girlfriend. Tomorrow you tell Beatrice that the author of her *famous* manuscript is alive and well in Denver.

Dora changed and went to bed, but as tired as she was, she still could not fall asleep. She concentrated on the sound of the water in the fountain outside. A while later, she was standing in the midst of a rain forest, watching her father parachute into a clearing a short distance from her. He was swinging his legs as if he were on a circus trapeze, laughing and waving at her. She was waving back, watching him somersault in the air, applauding. She was ten years old.

FIVE
Shades of Blues

THE AROMA OF FRESH-BREWED COFFEE stole through the door that separated Justin's living quarters from his agency office upstairs. With his eyes closed, he imagined Gloria making coffee, prioritizing activities and items, ready to start her workday. He, too, should get ready.

He opened his eyes when he realized it could not be Gloria upstairs. She was leaving for the Sierra Nevada for a few days of R & R. It was just a dream, he thought, as he looked at the clock by his bedside. It was only five in the morning.

Before he knew it, he had dozed off again. He was walking through an underground maze, like the Roman catacombs in Hollywood film epics he had seen about the persecution of Christians by Roman emperors. Except, oddly enough, sunlight streamed through holes in the roof of these tunnels. But where was he? And, all the people moving through sunlit glass tunnels, why were they going past him without so much as a glance in his direction? He was looking for someone, he knew.

The passage he traversed opened onto a courtyard, fenced on all four sides by tall hewn-stone walls. He looked for an exit, but there was none. He could only get out by going back the same way he had come in. By the time he stepped back into the tunnel, night had fallen. All he saw was a flash and for a split second the barrel of a gun. His eyes opened wide, focused on the blinding light. He felt no pain when the bullet went through his brain. Struggling to catch his breath, he woke up.

Upstairs, everything was quiet. Inside him, the silence was terrifyingly immense. He jumped out of bed, shaved, showered, and got dressed. He walked up the stairs. Something in the office seemed out of the ordinary. A torchiere lamp was slightly out of place, a file drawer not quite closed. Maybe Gloria really had come in early to do some work before driving up to the mountains.

He noticed the note on his desk; it was from her, dated the night before. "I'll be dropping a copy of a manuscript off at Art's Laney College office and another at Myra's house tomorrow morning. I'm hoping they might be able to tell me who the writer is. Too involved to tell you about it right now. Has to do with Dora's missing-person case. By the way, Dora might need a contact in Denver. I gave her Luis Móntez's number. Hope you don't mind. I'll call you from South Shore."

He stared blankly at the note for a while. Everything he thought about seemed trivial. He felt as if he were hungover, but he had not had even a beer since Elizabeth's party.

Elizabeth. He should call Highland Hospital. He turned, looking for the phone. He saw the photos of his sisters and of his parents on his desk, then looked at the wall calendar. Out of the blue, it seemed, he recalled the day his mother died. It dawned on him that his death dream that morning might have something to do with the approaching anniversary of his mother's death. Why the Roman catacombs otherwise? His mother loved to watch those Roman epics. He and his sisters had seen them all with her at one parochial school or another. This year, he promised himself, he would go to the cemetery with his sisters.

Back in his downstairs flat, he poured himself a glass of juice, then dialed Elizabeth's cell phone number.

"No change, so far," Elizabeth said as soon as she heard Justin's voice. "Gastón's sending someone to stay with Ramona while I go home. I'm taking a few days off from work. I'll call you as soon as Ramona regains consciousness."

After he hung up, Justin looked up the number of the Triple A office in Oakland. Before his friend Tito Figueroa went to work for the automobile association, he had worked for his father in his Bay Lock and Safe shop on Broadway. Justin hoped Tito could give him an idea on how to get information about the old key.

"Hey, man," Tito greeted him. "Haven't seen you in weeks. What you been up to?"

"Serving subpoenas, pursuing philandering husbands. Same ol', you know."

"Yeah, right. You're the only *vato* I know who gets paid to watch!" Tito said and laughed. "Got a new one," he continued, "Private dicks do it better when they watch. Watcha think?"

Justin smiled. Tito loved to come up with new slogans and jingles for commercial products or services, which he—unsuccessfully so far—tried to peddle to manufacturers from time to time.

"Not bad. A hundred bucks, maybe. But listen, man. I need your expertise. Problem with an old key. Do you think we can talk soon, maybe today?"

"Sure. Meet me at the Y at five thirty. Bring your racket. And get ready to lose. Then we'll talk," Tito said.

Wishing his friend good luck, Justin pressed the "off" button, then looked in his memo pad for the messenger delivery service phone and address. He punched the numbers and waited. After greeting the receptionist, he asked for Mitch Quintana, the owner. Quintana acknowledged that he had been expecting Justin's call. Gastón Saucedo had phoned earlier to authorize "the exchange of information between them." He spoke English well but with an unusual accent Justin could not quite place. Apologizing in advance for his rudeness, Mitch nonetheless asked Justin to furnish his P.I. license number. Justin did as told.

Satisfied, Mitch asked, "What would you like to know, Mr. Escobar?"

"Please, call me Justin. I'd like the name of your messenger and how to get a hold of him."

"José Ruiz Mendoza. Hang on. I'll put him on." While he waited for his employee to get on the line, Mitch added, "If you ever need our services, Justin, you know how to reach us."

"Sure do. Likewise. We're in the book—Brown Angel Security and Investigations. Thanks," Justin replied.

An instant later, José Ruiz Mendoza picked up the extension.

"Joe Mendoza, here. What would you like to know, Mr. Escobar?"

Sounding like someone who had been speaking English all his life, Mendoza seemed cautiously polite but pressed. Probably had a delivery to make, Justin assumed. "This is going to take some time. I'll treat you to a burger and fries for lunch."

"Can't do. Sorry. Lots to do. I'll be happy to answer your questions now."

"You sound like a cautious man. I mean, in your line of work, you must be, right?"

"It goes with the job," Joe replied in a perfunctory tone. "What exactly do you want to know?" His tone had become impatient, somewhat defiant.

Justin noticed the messenger's change in attitude, but he chose to ignore it. "All right. Bottom line. When you delivered the package to the woman at Vista Point, did you see anyone around, anything that seemed out of the ordinary?"

"Nothing."

Too short and too sweet. "Tell me exactly what you did when you got to Vista Point."

"I parked, walked to the car, and put the package on the backseat. That's all."

"Were there any other cars there, or on the way up to the area?"

"I didn't notice," Joe answered.

"And the woman waiting there, can you describe her?"

"She was standing there, with her back to me. I really didn't pay much attention. I delivered the envelope and got out of there. I had another delivery to make. Sorry."

"Quite all right. Thanks, anyway," Justin said.

Something was wrong. José Ruiz was being purposely evasive. What was going on, Justin wondered as he got in his van. He headed for the California State University-Hayward campus.

At the admissions office, Justin asked to speak to Muriel Ozuna.

The receptionist checked in a dog-eared campus directory. "I'm sorry, but I don't see her name anywhere," the young Japanese woman said. "Maybe Miss Vernan knows her. Just a moment." She reached for the phone and pressed the intercom button. "Miss Vernan, there's someone here looking for a Muriel Ozuna. I checked the campus listings but I don't see her name." After a few "Uh-huhs," she put the receiver back in its cradle. Pointing at the door to her left, she said,

"Go through that door. Miss Vernan will help you. Her office is the second door on your right as you go in."

Miss Vernan was waiting for him at the door. Justin introduced himself, trying to think quickly of a way to begin his inquiry.

Miss Vernan was a handsome African-American woman, probably in her early sixties. Her honey-colored eyes still sparkled in a way Justin had not seen even in women younger than she. Why the "Miss" title, he wondered, as he looked at her desk and saw the family photos, including one of two kids he assumed were her grandchildren. He caught a glimpse of another photo, a class photo, and his eyes lit up. He had found a way to put Miss Vernan at ease and broach the subject to her. He thanked his lucky stars.

Miss Vernan, who had been observing him, smiled, picked up the photo and showed it to him.

"What grade did you teach at Edna Brewer Middle School? I went to Glenview Elementary, then to McChesney Junior High, which, I understand, became Edna Brewer later," Justin commented.

"You're right. I transferred to Edna Brewer in 1980 when it was still McChesney Junior High. I taught English there until 1990. I loved those kids."

"I hope you don't mind my asking, but why did you quit?"

"A number of reasons. Parents lost their common sense. They delegated the responsibility for their children's education entirely to the educational system. Then they pointed the finger at us, the teachers, and accused us of not doing our job. To top it all, children can no longer speak without calling each other, even their teachers and parents, MFs or SOBs."

Justin chuckled. Once a teacher, always a teacher, he thought.

As if reading his mind, Miss Vernan said with a smile, "I know. Even now I can't bring myself to say those two awful expletives. Sadly, such language and all that violence are the reflection of what is happening with us as a society. Violence eats at young minds and hearts, like an infernal wasp. Children kill children. And we still think it's our teachers' fault. Remuneration, not to mention respect, for the teaching profession has dwindled. I couldn't bear such dismal conditions any longer and I stopped doing what I loved most."

She was lost in thought as she looked at the class photo. A moment later, she added, "But I'm sure you didn't come in to talk about the vicissitudes of teachers. You're looking for Muriel Ozuna, Jenny informed me."

"Do you know her?"

"Indeed I do. May I ask what your business with her is?"

Justin did not answer right away. Miss Vernan impressed him as a straightforward, fair-minded person. He was certain he could trust her, so he decided to be candid with her.

"I'm actually interested in locating Mr. Ozuna. A twelve-month-old baby girl's life depends on my finding him. She needs a bone marrow transplant. Mr. Ozuna is her last hope," he explained and paused to give Miss Vernan a chance to process his request. He did not have to wait long.

"Is the baby his—Willie's?" she asked.

"A grandchild, I believe."

"My goodness! This is all news . . . Uh. Poor Muriel. She keeps finding out things about her husband, even now. Not only was he not a graduate of Cal. . . . Was he ever honest? It's almost as if she had been married to Dr. Jekyll and Mr. Hyde. I personally never liked the man. Secretive. A wolf in sheep's clothing. I never really knew what he did for a living. Whatever it was, there wasn't enough money in it to support his family. Or so he claimed."

"You speak of him in the past, is he . . . ?"

"Dead? No. It would have been kinder of him to die. At least Muriel could get his pension, if any. But no. She finally saw him for what he was and left him. You have to understand, Muriel is one of the most gentle, trusting souls I've ever known. Theirs was an interracial marriage. You might not know this, but Willie is a black Puerto Rican, which, in the end, has little to do with his lack of responsibility. Nonetheless, it was not easy for her and her children, who look like him more than her. We always think about racism being a one-way street to injustice, but it actually is a two-way road. Nothing good comes of it, either way. But amazingly, when she finally told Willie she'd had enough, he let her go. By that time, their two sons were grown up."

"Do you happen to know where Willie is now?"

"I'm not really sure, but recently Muriel mentioned that he sent a birthday card to one of their sons with a hundred-dollar bill in it. It was posted somewhere in Oakland."

"Posted in Oakland? Where does Mrs. Ozuna live?"

"I'm sorry, Mr. Escobar. I thought I'd mentioned that Muriel moved to Florida after their divorce. Her mother lives there. Muriel takes care of her."

"Would you mind telling me how I can get in touch with Mrs. Ozuna?" Justin asked, then quickly added, "Or perhaps she might prefer to get in touch with me. She can call me at any of these phone numbers during the day. Or at my cell phone number any time, day or night." Justin handed Miss Vernan his business card.

"I owe her a call. I think it's better if I pass on your request and phone numbers to her," Miss Vernan said. She extended her right hand towards Justin.

Shaking the hand offered, Justin said, "I'm really grateful for all your help."

"Don't mention it, Mr. Escobar. I do hope you find Willie and he does the right thing for that precious baby girl."

SIX
Lavender Lies

"MY BROTHER VINCENT SPEAKS ENGLISH perfectly well. He doesn't have an accent. It can't be him on the . . ." Beatrice didn't finish her sentence. She looked at Dora, who was staring at her in disbelief. "I'm sorry. I should have told you before."

"Your brother Vincent? My God!" Dora said as she tried to process quickly what Beatrice had unwittingly let out. "Are you saying that this missing writer is your brother Vincent? Why in. . . . Damn!" She shook her head repeatedly. "So you didn't find the manuscript at the dump like you told me."

"Yes, I did. I did," Beatrice said vehemently. "It was the lavender paper, see? My brother uses that color paper for a first rough draft of a story. I showed it to him. He told me it was his, but that he wasn't interested in writing that story anymore. He was writing it for a woman. She was more trouble than it was worth to him, he said. He threw it away. I found it at the dump. Then . . . he disappeared. He left a note. A key to his safe for me. If anything happened to him I should look in his safe. Everything would become clear. But he didn't tell me where the safe is. A man will surrender the key to his safe to a trusted friend when his life is in danger. I read that in a novel. He's dead, isn't he? Vincent is dead."

Beatrice was breathless. Her eyes shone and moved rapidly from side to side as if she were looking for an avenue of escape. She looked very fragile and distraught.

"Slow down. It's all right," Dora said and held her for a while. "I'm going to call this Jesse Latour in Denver. Maybe he knows your

33

brother Vincent. Maybe your brother is pretending to be this man. Don't worry. Go in and get me a photo of Vincent, the most recent one. I'll wait for you here. Go on."

Beatrice did as told. She came back with two photos, none of them very clear. She described her brother as being of average height and build, olive skin, having brown hair and hazel eyes, and a long scar right above his right eyebrow.

"Please," Dora begged of Beatrice, "Don't spoon-feed me the information I need to find your brother. I cannot do my job with a hand tied behind my back."

"I won't do it anymore. I promise."

Dora walked back into her house and immediately headed for the office. She dialed the number for Palabras con Sabor Coffeehouse in Denver. She asked to talk to Jesse Latour. When he picked up the call, she said, "Look. I don't know what your business with Vincent Constantino is, but I need to talk with him. I know you know him. Tell him his sister Beatrice wants him to call her. *¿Me entiendes?*"

"She sen joo. Say her. She come here. No deal," Latour said.

"Look. You keep saying 'she.' Who's she? I don't know the woman you're talking about. *¿Quién es la mujer? ¿Cómo se llama?*"

Latour hung up on her. She'd hardly put the receiver back in its cradle when the phone rang again. She expected to hear Latour's voice, but the caller was Gloria.

"You sound upset. What's happening?" Gloria asked.

Dora explained briefly what had transpired since the previous evening.

"And you think Vincent and this Latour are one and the same?"

"I don't know what to think. This guy in Denver can hardly speak English. Beatrice mentioned that Vincent was writing the book for someone else, possibly a woman. Maybe Vincent, maybe this mysterious woman, is writing Latour's story. I'm not exactly sure what that means," Dora said.

"Vincent might be what's called a ghostwriter. Some people hire a writer and they tell him or her about their lives. Then the writer writes a first-person narrative based on the information provided by the person who hired him," Gloria explained. "Celebrities usually do that."

"I see. Clever," Dora said. "But what happens if either the writer or the client wants to take full credit?"

"Then they have a conflict of interest. They usually sign a contract, though. Do you think that's the case with those two?"

"How the hell would I know! Beatrice thinks that Vincent is writing the book for a woman. This guy in Denver keeps talking about a woman. He wants her to meet with him in person or no deal."

"A woman? From Oakland?"

"Possibly. Agghh! I feel like I'm a player in a *telenovela*. You know, one of those convoluted TV night soaps, teeming with family intrigue and virulent relationships."

Gloria burst out laughing at the other end. When she quieted down, she said, "Why don't you call Luis Móntez, Justin's attorney friend in Denver? I gave you his phone number yesterday. Justin says it's okay to use him as reference. Luis Móntez might know a photographer there who might be able to take a photo of Latour. If Vincent is Latour, you'll at least have proof that he's alive and in Denver. That's what I'd do if I were you."

"Hey, that's an idea. I might do that. Then I suppose I'll have to go to Denver and get Vincent. I have some miles with United, enough to get a free round trip ticket to Denver. I'd hoped to go to New Mexico for Christmas. Grrr. I hate this," Dora said, gathering her abundant curly black hair and raising it to fan the nape of her neck with her hand. "I'm sorry to burden you with my troubles. How I wish I could go with you to South Shore, instead of this. . . . Hell! What time are you leaving?"

"I'm picking up my mom at one. I already dropped the copies of the manuscript off at Art's college office and at Myra Miranda's house this morning. Art said he and Myra will get to it today. He asked if you'd be free this evening to have dinner at his house at six. Then the three of you can talk about it. I tentatively told him you'd do that. Should I call him back and confirm or cancel?"

"I'll be there," Dora said. "They might be able to help me identify the woman who hired Vincent. Every little bit helps."

After giving Dora directions to Art's house, Gloria said good-bye. Dora looked for Luis Móntez's number in Denver. He wasn't in, so she left a message in his voice mail detailing her request. She would be happy to wire him the money for the photographer's services.

While she waited for Móntez to call back, she decided to clean her closet. She'd been meaning to give away some old clothes. She looked carefully at the large number of linen and silk blouses ruined by a variety of stains, from coffee to catsup and other reminders of hasty meals as she watched for philandering husbands to leave the dwelling of their mistresses. The pathetic state of her wardrobe had prompted her to ask her tax accountant if she could deduct her clothing expenses from her tax liability. After all, she had ruined her clothing in the course of her profession. Her accountant had burst her bubble with a "Let me put it to you this way. Even Liberace had a hard time convincing the IRS he needed his costumes for his performances, and so did the King." So that was that.

After two hours and three piles of stained clothes on her bedroom floor, her skin was beginning to itch. A sure sign that she was reaching critical stress. Patience was not one of her virtues. The best thing was to work out her anxiety. A session at the pool would do her good. A few laps always helped to clear her mind. She gathered her swimwear and headed for the YMCA.

As soon as she was in the water, she knew she had made the right decision. Swimming was the kind of sport she loved most to watch and do. To move in the water with grace and confidence, like her father, was something she wished she could do. Chuck Saldaña had trained as a Navy Seal and had been with the team for a few years. He believed she was good enough to swim for her high school team, and he encouraged her to join it.

"Like all the other elements, water has its own rhythm, its own power. Feel it. Go with it. Never fight an undertow. Find the current that will take you safely to shore. All conditions being somewhat equal, you can use its power to your advantage. It's up to you," her father had told her often. He also reminded her that the same principle applied to self-defense. "Use your opponent's force to your advantage." He taught her well. Of his three children, she had been his star pupil.

Dora knew, however, that with all the effort and practice she had put into swimming over the years, she should be a much more efficient, faster swimmer. She had to admit she would never be a great swimmer, but that did not have to keep her from enjoying herself.

After Dora finished her laps, she went into the sauna to sweat out the pool smell. She took a quick shower, got dressed, and headed for her car, which was parked in the garage behind the Y.

She was driving down the exit ramp when she saw Justin Escobar take the up ramp. She waved at him, but he did not see her. A man in a blue polo shirt with the YMCA letters printed on its front pocket was walking down the center of the exit ramp. When Dora saw him, she slammed on her brakes and came within inches of hitting him. The man approached her car, glared at her, then pounded her car with his fist. Dora was not about to find out how far his anger would push him. She revved the engine, staring at him all the while. Surprised at her gesture of defiance, the man jumped out of her way. She hastened down the exit, her heart screeching inside her chest as loud as the tires on the pavement.

She parked and took a deep breath to steady her nerves. As she was getting ready to start up again, she saw Justin heading towards the entrance to the YMCA. The man she saw in the parking lot followed Justin at a discreet distance. Justin stopped to tie one of his shoes. The man hid behind a car. He started up again when Justin did.

Dora drove around the block to the entrance of the YMCA, parked in a yellow zone, and went up the steps. She saw Justin in line to check in while the man shadowing him asked to be buzzed in and busied himself picking up some soiled towels by the desk. He glanced at Justin every so often. Then he headed down the stairs towards the locker room ahead of Justin.

No doubt about it, paranoia was an occupational hazard for private and public cops alike, she well knew. But Gloria had told her that she and Justin were not working on any particular case. And something about the whole episode kept nagging at her. Justin, on the other hand, seemed quite relaxed. He was a trained professional, quite able to take care of himself, she decided. She walked back to her car and headed home to change for her dinner appointment with Art Bello and Myra Miranda. She would come up with an excuse to call Justin later, make sure he was all right, and warn him he had drawn a shadow.

SEVEN
Shadow at the Y

AT FIVE IN THE AFTERNOON, Oakland's YMCA Downtown was a very busy place. Justin waited in line for a while, paid his fee for the day, and headed down the stairs towards the men's locker room. At the bottom of the stairs, he turned a corner and bumped into an African-American man standing just across from the locker room door. The guy was wearing a blue shirt with the Y's logo on it.

Justin apologized and the man grinned, baring a set of tobacco-stained teeth. While Justin changed, he saw the man come in and stand by the door of the locker room. There was something odd about him, something out of the ordinary, but Justin could not quite figure out what it was.

His friend, Tito Figueroa, was already warming up at the racquetball court. After a brief greeting, they began to play. For the next half hour, they concentrated on the game, taking short rests every so often. During one of those breaks, Justin felt himself being observed and looked up at the large windows overlooking the courts. He caught only a glimpse of a blue shirtsleeve that quickly disappeared behind the observation deck wall.

Their session finished, he and Tito walked back to the locker room. The African-American attendant Justin had seen earlier handed them towels as they entered.

"Do you know this guy?" Justin asked Tito.

His friend shook his head. "Why?"

"Nothing, really. Something about him seems familiar."

Justin headed towards the sauna while Tito walked to the shower area. They agreed to meet at the snack bar upstairs, next to the reception counter.

Tito was already drinking from a Gatorade bottle when Justin joined him. Justin took out the photocopies of the key and the photo of the man Elizabeth thought was her daughter Irene's father. He handed Tito the copy of the key that had been stolen from Ramona's car.

Tito looked at it carefully, and said, "I'm not sure, but this looks like the key to a safe. This type of safe featured a code mechanism and a lock. They were made by Masterlock. The company went belly-up about ten years ago. They almost exclusively made security and safety equipment for federal agencies. The two guys who owned the company both died in a plane crash. Their sons took over the company, but they were always at each other's throats. The government warned them, but they just couldn't work things out. Finally, the government withdrew its contracts and Masterlock filed for chapter eleven."

"What you're telling me is that there's no way to trace this key," Justin said.

"Not exactly. But it might take me a while. How soon do you need the info?"

"Sooner," Justin answered.

"I'll see what I can do." Tito got up to leave.

"Take the copies with you. It's an extra set."

Tito reached for the papers on the table. He realized he had also picked up the man's photos and handed them back to Justin.

Justin was about to put Willie Oz's photos back in his sports bag, but he stopped. He looked at the image of the young Puerto Rican in it. "Can't be." He bolted to his feet and quickly headed back to the stairs leading to the men's locker room. "Call me!" he yelled back to Tito.

Justin pushed open the door to the locker room slowly. He checked the showers, sauna, and steam rooms, the pool, and finally the gym, courts, and track upstairs. There was no sign of the man with the tobacco-stained teeth, so Justin took a strategic position outside the staff room. While many employees went in and out of it, the attendant he was looking for remained at large. He was almost sure that man was Willie Oz. But how had Oz found him? Justin cursed under his breath. If Oz had been at Vista Point and had taken the envelope from Ramona's car after pushing her over the rail, he would, of course, have Justin's address.

He stopped at a Starbucks and got a latte to drink on his way home. The coffee was hot and burned his lips, so he removed the lid and put the cup in the cup holder. All the way home he kept an eye out for Willie Oz, uselessly, since he did not know what kind of vehicle the man drove.

Justin drove up his driveway fast and the coffee in the full cup splashed, spilling onto the stick gear shaft and the edge of the passenger seat. He got out of his van to retrieve a rag from his toolbox in the back to clean the spill. He was about to open the rear door when his cell phone rang. The mess would have to wait. He pushed the talk button on his phone and greeted the caller.

"How're you doing, partner?"

He recognized Dora's voice. "Well as can be. How about you? Wassup?" A pause at the other end.

"Listen. I might be wrong, but I think you're being tailed," Dora said, then described what she saw at the Y earlier and her suspicions about the man.

"I'm aware of it now. Thanks for the warning."

"Anything I can do?"

"Nothing at this time. I'll call you if I need your help. Thanks for the offer."

As he clicked his phone off, his eyes swept the area around him. Oz was nowhere near him. Who was he dealing with? According to Miss Vernan, Oz was a wolf in sheep's clothing.

Justin retrieved a rag from his toolbox and a bottle of Windex he kept there and began to clean the seat, then reached in to check the gear shaft. His fingers brushed against a tiny antenna-like protrusion. He retrieved his hand quickly as if he had just touched a roach. He hated roaches. He got the rag in his hand ready to squash the bug, but none ran out. Pulling apart the cover, he saw the tiny metallic object taped onto the lining. It was a bug, all right, but not the kind you find in a pantry. Who else but Oz, he concluded. The man following him was a lot more resourceful than an old revolutionary, resting on past laurels. He was about to pull out the electronic device but decided to leave it be. He would use it to his advantage by letting Oz foster the illusion that he still had the upper hand.

To be on the safe side, Justin checked his van thoroughly, but found no other bugs. He jumped back in and headed for Highland Hospital. Elizabeth had a lot of explaining to do.

EIGHT
Woman in Question

DORA DROVE UP SERPENTINE MANDANA ROAD toward the Oakland hills. Further up, a sign announced that she was entering the city of Piedmont, an island of wealth, surrounded on all sides by Oakland proper. Mansions rose at the end of long driveways, meadow-like lawns and gardens with fountains in their midst, all partially hidden behind tall hedges.

She followed Mandana Road up to the home of Sara Saenz Owens, a well-known photographer and banker's widow. Art Bello rented a guest cottage from Mrs. Owens. The house was surrounded by gardens, two acres of oaks and California pines. Art's cottage was about fifty feet from the main house, next to the pool and its facilities.

Dora parked next to a 1964 red Mustang. She got out and pushed the car door closed. She marveled at the gardens. The yellows and pinks of February and March had made room also for lavenders and mixed blues and reds, an orgy of color for her eyes, and a feast of nectar for hummingbirds and butterflies come June. She heard voices and followed them to the bamboo-fenced lanai next to the house. Art and Myra greeted her warmly. She and Myra talked for a while about everything and nothing while Art went back into the house to check on dinner.

During dinner, the conversation mostly centered around her friendship with Gloria and their line of work. After dinner, Myra reached for her copy of the manuscript and began to talk about it.

"This author is self-conscious. Either he's a beginning writer or he's trying very hard to fictionalize something that defies counterfeiting," Myra commented.

"I'm assuming you're sure the author is a man," Dora said.

"Not really. Actually, as I was reading through it, I had the feeling that a woman had written certain parts of it. The narrative voice changes during moments of reflection. The sex scene, I'm almost certain, was written by a man. I don't know how to explain it. Male authors seem to describe sexual scenes in more graphic, physical ways. Women writers are more concerned with the way good—or bad—sex feels, the feelings they experience during the act itself. And to tell you the truth, in this case, I'm not sure how the woman feels. Every so often, I got the feeling that she wasn't much into it, or that maybe . . . the guy was forcing himself on her?"

Turning to Art, Myra asked, "What's your take on all this?"

"I agree with you. I'd go as far as saying that what's being described here is a rape—could be a date rape." Turning to Dora, Art asked, "Where did you find this manuscript and why is it important?" Before Dora had a chance to explain, he added, "The reason I'm asking is that there are a lot of details about things that happened during the Third World Student Strike at Berkeley in 1969. Things that only someone who lived through it could know. This author, whoever he or she is, was there."

"I don't think he was. My client believes the author of this manuscript is her brother, and he's missing, possibly in danger."

"So you know who he is."

"All I know is that he told my client that he was writing the story for a woman," Dora said. "His name is Vincent Constantino."

"Never heard of him," Art said and looked at Myra. "Have you?"

Myra shook her head. "Who could the woman be, though? We were at Berkeley, all through the Third World Student Strike, the anti-Vietnam War demonstrations, People's Park, and up to the Cambodian crisis. But I never heard of any Chicanita being raped back then. 'Free love' and drugs, plenty of those. Whether we liked it or not, we were a generation influenced in one way or another by the flower children. No question about it. But I don't remember hearing even a rumor about a Chicana being raped, especially while the fuzz was beating the hell out of us just a few blocks away."

Art raised his eyebrows and nodded. "Not that it couldn't have happened." He tapped his lips with his index finger, then added, "Some of the passages ring so true. I know I've read them before. I just can't remember where, how long ago, or who wrote them."

"You don't mean Delia Treviño or Jeff Morones," Myra inquired.

"No, I'm not talking about Delia. Her style is very different. And Jeff is a poet, not a novelist," Art replied.

Myra agreed with a smile.

"Who are those two?" Dora asked.

"They were students at Berkeley at the time of the strike. Actually, Jeff's story is an interesting one," Myra said. "He was suspected of being an FBI plant."

"Was he?" Dora asked, intrigued.

"Of course not," Art said. "We were all so paranoid then. For good reasons, though. The feds and the city cops infiltrated every organization that even smacked of, quote, "radical," unquote, back then. Jeff wasn't one of them."

"But since we're on the subject. There were a couple of guys who might have been undercover cops," Myra said and paused. "I can't think of their names now. You know who I'm talking about, Art? I used to call them the Dynamic Duo, always trying to convince us to 'zap and pow' the cops, always preaching violence. One of them tried to join the Black Panthers. As a matter of fact, I think he did, but the Panthers threw him out. So did the Brown Berets. Remember?"

Art frowned. "I know who you're talking about. I have their names on the tip of my tongue . . ."

"See? I keep telling you," Myra remarked, "we're beginning to forget a lot of what happened then."

"No shit!" Art replied. To Dora, he said, "Anyway, if someone gave me something to read that resembles the writing in your manuscript, I'm sure I have a copy of it in my files."

"I hate to impose, but, any chance you might look in your files for it soon?" Dora asked.

"No trouble. I'm curious myself. And I've been meaning to clear a couple of my file drawers. Tomorrow is Saturday, as good a day as any. I'll call you as soon as I have news for you. Gloria gave me your number, but write it down for me, just in case."

Dora reached for her handbag, pulled out her memo pad, and wrote her cell and home phone numbers on it. She tore the slip off and handed it to Art.

"Call me, too, Art," Myra requested. "I'd love to find out who wrote this. You know, bro', we really should try to write about our experiences at Berkeley back then, before senility sets in." She laughed.

"You do it. I'll be your critic and editor," Art said half in jest. "I don't think I can revisit Berkeley in the sixties yet. In the wake of the English Only and anti-Bilingual Ed initiatives and the end of affirmative action by the U.C. Regents, I'd be afraid to confirm how . . ."

"How much of our bloody souls we left there and for what?" Myra said, completing Art's statement.

"Damn right! We seemed to have gained so little for the next generations of Chicanos. I don't have the nerve to write about our failures. Too painful to go into that inferno even for a poet."

Dora listened for a while about their experiences at Berkeley. Near ten o'clock she thanked them for their efforts on her behalf and left. On her way home, she checked her voice mail, hoping that Luis Móntez had called. He had. He was acquainted with Palabras con Sabor and knew the owners of the coffeehouse. He could make discreet inquiries about Jesse Latour and take a photo of the man himself. He and Dora could talk about expenses later. He needed her e-mail address so he could scan the photos and send them to her. She called his office number in Denver and left a message, accepting his offer and giving him her e-mail address.

Luis Móntez was either a very nice guy or he had a lot of respect and affection for Justin Escobar.

By the time Dora reached her home, she had decided to accept Justin and Gloria's offer to be the third partner in Brown Angel Security and Investigations.

NINE
Further Compromises

AN OPAL MOON navigated through a lock of night as Justin pulled into the parking lot at Highland Hospital. He had called Elizabeth and asked her to meet him in the waiting area on the first floor. Grilling Elizabeth about Oz was not something he looked forward to. He turned off the engine but stayed in his van. A brown van pulled into a spot in the row behind him. A blue sheriff's hospital security patrol cruised down the lot in front of him. No one got out of the brown vehicle. He looked in the rear-view mirror. It was a Dodge van, but he could not make out the license numbers and letters in the dim light. It had to be Oz. At least now he knew the kind of vehicle the man was driving.

Justin waited a little while longer, keeping an eye on the Dodge van. He debated with himself whether he should tell Elizabeth that Oz was following him. He knew Oz was aware of his moves because the man had planted a listening device in his van. But who had told Oz that he was looking for him to begin with? Possibly Miss Vernan had called Muriel Ozuna and Muriel had informed Willie Oz. Possibly, but not probably. It did not make sense. He had seen Miss Vernan just that morning. He had been in his van most of the day, giving Oz very narrow windows of opportunity to deal with the van alarm and plant the bug in it. If Oz had planted the bug in such a short time, he was a pro. A professional what? P.I.? Car burglar? Someone had the answers to his questions. Elizabeth and her husband Gastón topped that list.

He walked into the hospital and headed directly to the men's restroom. Just in case, he searched his clothes, his cell phone, wallet, and even his key ring for other listening devices. He found none, so he

45

went up to the waiting area. Elizabeth was already there. She looked exhausted but she smiled at him. She took him by the hand and led him to a pair of empty seats.

Justin inquired immediately about Ramona's condition. Earlier in the evening, Ramona's eyes had fluttered open once but closed again. The doctors had told Elizabeth not to get her hopes up, that it might not mean anything. Perhaps all that muscle activity meant a further compromise of Ramona's nervous system.

"Maybe, just maybe, she's trying very hard to wake up," Elizabeth said. She covered a yawn with her hand. "How is it going with you?"

"Little progress," Justin said and related his conversation with Miss Vernan about Muriel Ozuna and with the messenger José Mendoza. "A friend is helping me to identify the Masterlock key. He thinks it's a key to a safe." Justin paused and watched Elizabeth's reaction. She seemed to be listening but offered no hint of pleasure or displeasure at the news. "Do you have any idea where this Masterlock safe might be?"

"I don't know anything about any safe. I had no idea Willie had one. Maybe you should ask Muriel Ozuna. Maybe she has it." Elizabeth yawned again and she rubbed the nape of her neck. "Would you mind getting me some coffee? I'm about to drop, I'm so tired."

Justin went to look for a vending machine. When he got back to the waiting area, Gastón Saucedo was there, talking with his wife. He was clad in a stylish suit and tie, and sported a recently cropped head of brown hair with white streaks along the temples. He was the perfect picture of business elegance. He rose about a head above Elizabeth, who was by no means a short woman, and who seemed quite upset at the moment.

Neither of them took notice of Justin's presence near them.

"You'll have to do it. Tell her," Justin overheard Gastón say to his wife. Elizabeth shook her head, denying his request.

When Gastón saw Justin standing nearby, he turned his attention to him. "The press has gotten wind of some rumor or another. A car was parked outside the house for a while earlier this evening. My security people just told me that the same car is parked there as we speak. I was just telling Elizabeth to expect them to show up here soon."

"And your security people are sure this individual is a reporter," Justin inquired.

"It seemed obvious to them. The man was snapping pictures of our house. When my people went out to question him, he backed off, but they noticed he was wearing a press tag. Unfortunately, he took off in a hurry. But he's back now."

"With all due respect, Mr. Saucedo, I wouldn't take it for granted this individual is a reporter, regardless of his camera and ID." Justin got not only Gastón's but Elizabeth's full attention.

Elizabeth looked at Gastón, who glanced in his wife's direction but immediately took his eyes off hers. Justin could not decipher the glance that passed between husband and wife. Brief as it was, Gastón's eyes were filled with apprehension.

Elizabeth raised her hand and rubbed her forehead with it. "Is he . . . do you think this man has something to do with Ramona's acc . . . ?"

"I don't know. Maybe with Willie Oz. But I wouldn't take any chances." Justin looked in Gastón's eyes. He seemed quite calm and collected by then.

Elizabeth gave Justin a blank look.

Why weren't they delighted that Oz might be near at hand? Did they fear that Oz would turn down their request to be tested for bone marrow compatibility? Or were they afraid that Irene might find out who her real father was, perhaps turning against her mother?

"Should I have my people question this . . . reporter?" Gastón looked at Elizabeth who did not respond. Turning to Justin, he said, "My wife wanted to wait until Ramona regains consciousness. She still wants to . . ."

Gastón stopped in mid-sentence and turned to look at his wife, who was squeezing his arm. Justin saw Saucedo stare at her in what he perceived as confusion. Elizabeth's cheeks flushed. Suspicion swept through Justin's mind, and he had to suppress an impulse to pursue the matter further. Better to wait, he decided, see what kind of hand he was being dealt.

Gastón's cell phone rang. He moved to the side to take the call. Muttering something about a crisis at his nightclub, he kissed Elizabeth good-bye and rushed out.

Saved by the bell, Justin thought of Saucedo's quick exit. Elizabeth took a few steps as if she were ready to leave, then turned back to face Justin.

"I can't tell you just yet what's going on, but I can assure you it has nothing to do with your investigation. I still want Willie Oz found and tested for compatibility."

"I want to believe you. But from what Miss Vernan told me about Oz, he's led a double life for a long time. He's got to be a master of deception, a pro. He's not an aging, frustrated revolutionary, or wannabe, as you put it, is he?"

"I don't know. I already told you all I know about him," Elizabeth answered.

"All right. Let's go back to the beginning. Before and after the delivery of the envelope, did you tell someone that you'd hired me to find Oz? Who else besides Ramona, you, or your husband knew about it?"

"I already told you all about it," Elizabeth said a bit miffed.

"What about, let's say, your daughters Irene and Serena. Do they know? Could they have mentioned it to someone else?"

"Irene knows nothing, nothing about this. Serena is very curious and she might have overheard Gastón and me talk about some things, but not about Willie Oz, not about the delivery at Vista Point or who you are. She wasn't even home the night of the party at our house. Gastón and I thought it best to keep both of them out of this as much as possible." Elizabeth paused. "I can't think of anybody else who might have known about Vista Point. Other than Mitch Quintana, but he's very loyal to Gastón. I don't think Gastón even told him why we needed to find Willie Oz."

"Maybe Mitch is loyal to your husband. I'm not sure about Quintana's messenger. Do you know him?"

"I don't. But what about him?"

"Just a gut feeling. When I talked to him on the phone, he seemed evasive. I think I'm going to pay Mendoza a visit, first thing tomorrow."

Justin got up to leave. "By the way, call me on my cell phone when you need to reach me. I'll be on the move all day tomorrow."

When he reached the parking lot, he looked for the brown Dodge van. It was gone.

TEN
A Harbor in View

IT WAS A GLORIOUS SPRING SATURDAY, so why did she feel so depressed? Dora asked herself as she looked out her office window. She had waited for news from either Art Bello or from Luis Móntez in Denver. Then she had served a couple of subpoenas and had picked up her tax returns at her accountant's office, gone over them and mailed them. She had made just enough in 1999 to meet all of her expenses and put some money into a tax shelter annuity. A quick review of her tax returns indicated she was getting a small reimbursement from the state and a somewhat larger one from the IRS. She sighed. She sure hoped she would fare better after she started working at Brown Angel.

She cleaned the kitchen and bathroom, then made herself a sandwich and downed it with a glass of iced tea in her office. She watched Beatrice cleaning the courtyard and fountain and tending to the roses. She toyed with the idea of going out to the yard and chatting with her client, as she had done many times before. But she knew the conversation would inevitably turn to the subject at hand. She had nothing new to report.

She watched the late morning TV newscast instead, but soon got tired of hearing all about homicides, the first forest fire of the season in Southern California, and the car pile-ups on various highways. She turned the TV off, read for a while, then cleaned the gun her father had left her.

A couple of hours later, she heard the beep indicating that she had e-mail. She logged on and was happy to read the note from Luis Móntez in Denver, advising her he had located Jesse Latour, who had shown up that morning at Palabras con Sabor. Luis had been able to snap a couple of photos of him. The owners of the coffeehouse had said that Latour had not been living in Denver long. He was from somewhere in South America, but they were not sure which city or country. Latour had indicated that he had been born in the United States but had lived most of his life abroad. He had recently obtained a Social Security number, which confirmed that he most likely had been straightforward about his birth.

Dora downloaded and printed the photos Luis had sent. "I sure hope you know where Vincent Constantino is," she said to the man in the photos, a redhead with a ruddy complexion, perhaps in his early thirties. Latour sat in an easy chair, hunched over a newspaper. It was hard to ascertain his height. He wore a heavy dark-brown jacket and khaki pants, making it difficult to determine his build as well.

She took the computer-generated photos with her and went out to look for Beatrice. She rapped softly on her client's window. Beatrice peeked out from behind the curtains. Dora signaled for her to join her. She went back to her office, leaving the front door open for Beatrice, who arrived a few minutes later.

"Do you know this guy?" Dora asked, showing her the photos.

Beatrice studied the photos, then shook her head.

"Are you sure? Take a good look," Dora insisted.

"I don't. Who is he? You sound upset. What's happening? Did he kidnap my brother, is that it?" Beatrice said in her usual rapid-fire style.

Dora smiled. "I don't know. I don't think so. But he might be able to tell us where we can find Vincent." She was finally learning how to speak with Beatrice without getting annoyed with her.

"What are we going to do now?" Beatrice asked Dora in a sub-dued tone.

Her client was now thinking as "we," not "you." Dora doubted she would have that much control over Beatrice, should her client decide to act on her own.

"I . . . I am going to call Art Bello later. Maybe he has news about the woman who hired Vincent to write her story. Patience. I'll let you know as soon as I find out. All right?"

Beatrice agreed with a nod. "Sharon and I are volunteering at the bingo game at four. It's a fund-raiser for the homeless. If you have any news, would you beep me? I'll take my pager with me. *Y yo te llamo pa'trás.*" She went back to the main house.

An hour later, Dora got a call from Art Bello. He had come across something written by a friend of his, a woman, a long time ago. He and Myra wanted to compare both manuscripts to be sure. He would call Dora as soon as he had something more concrete to tell her.

She felt restless, having little to do but wait. She looked through her video collection and pulled out *Moonstruck.* Nothing better than a romantic comedy with two of her favorite actors, Cher and Nicolas Cage. Soon she was totally immersed in the characters' romantic problems. Thank God for the movies, she thought as she propped her pillow up and rested her head on it.

Two hours later, as she rewound the tape, a what-if idea struck her. Why had she not thought of it before? If there was a safe, as Beatrice had indicated earlier, it had to be somewhere in Vincent's apartment on Harbor View. Beatrice would be back at eight that evening, early enough to call Vincent's landlord and make arrangements. What was in Vincent's safe? If lucky, she would find out the reason for his disappearance and information about his whereabouts; if not, at least she would know the identity of the mysterious woman who had hired him to write her tale of activism and sexual misfortune.

ELEVEN
Day Laborers and Urban Vaquero

MENDOZA, THE MESSENGER WHO HAD delivered the package to Ramona at Vista Point, was very reluctant to talk at first. But Justin insisted, calmly and firmly, leaning on the driver's door of the messenger's station wagon.

"I wish I could help you. But . . . I need my job." Mendoza was beginning to sweat.

Justin insisted. "Look, I'm not here to make trouble for you. It's all strictly confidential. I'll keep you out of it as much as possible. You have my word. But think about this. If the police get involved, you won't have a chance to hold on to your job." Justin looked directly into Mendoza's eyes.

Mendoza held his breath, then exhaled. "*El marido de mi hermana*, my brother-in-law, he beats my sister and takes the little she makes as a waitress. *Luego va y se la cura*. He sucks it all up his nose. I got a call from my sister that day. I just wanted to make sure my sister was okay. She needed me. So I went to her place to take her and her kids to my house. My brother-in-law was there. He had a knife. I gave him five-hundred dollars, all my savings, to get him to leave."

The messenger's tone of urgency convinced Justin he was telling the truth. Justin looked in his wallet for a business card to offer the guy. It was from a support group and shelter that a friend had just started for abused Latino women and their children over in the Fruitvale barrio. The shelter was also sponsored and watched over by the Chicano Peace Officers Association of Fruitvale. "Here. *Llama*. They might be able to help your sister, if she really wants help. Tell them I referred you."

Mendoza was impressed with Justin's unsolicited offer to help. "My friend Fermín Castro made the delivery for me. I trust him," he said. He took out a notepad and wrote a note to Fermín, asking him to cooperate with Justin. He handed the note to Justin. "Fermín hangs around the old Montgomery Ward on International Boulevard and Twenty-ninth Avenue. He always wears black clothes and black-and-white cow's hair boots."

Justin looked at his watch. It was ten in the morning. "It's Saturday. Do you think he'll be there?"

"Oh, sure. Just about now would be a good time to find him there."

As Justin walked to his van, he noticed the brown Dodge van parked half a block away. Oz was back on his tail. If Oz wanted a confrontation with him, he already had plenty of opportunities to make it happen. So what did Oz hope to gain by following him? It was better to string Oz along, Justin decided, as he made his way to the old Montgomery Ward building. He would choose the time and place for their confrontation.

Twenty minutes later, Justin arrived at the old Montgomery Ward. He parked in the Goodwill Industries thrift store across from the building. Oz drove his van into the parking lot of "La Bodega," a furniture store kitty-corner from Ward's.

Looking to spot Fermín Castro, Justin let his eyes wander through the throng of Mexican workers lining the sidewalk at the old Ward's site. When the retail store had closed its doors for good, its catalogue department remained open for a few years. Afterwards, vandalized and tagged, the building stood as an abandoned monstrosity for two decades. It had been used as a crack house, a dump, a place for homeless people, and a meeting place for gangs. It was now a great cause of controversy. Some city council members wanted the old store torn down to build a sorely needed elementary school in the area, while some Oakland residents wanted it preserved as a historical site.

Elizabeth had been among those pushing for demolition. Had she unwittingly stepped on someone's political toes? Was Oz actively involved in the controversy? Hard to say.

While city officials and preservationists argued in favor or against demolition, a large group of unemployed Mexican workers had begun gathering on the sidewalks around the building every morning. They hoped to get picked out for temporary jobs by prospective employers driving up and down the very busy International Boulevard and parallel East Twelfth Street.

Justin saw a pickup truck pull up to the curb. It was immediately surrounded by several men. As the employer drove away with his pick of the day, the other men went back to their places along the walls to wait for the next prospect.

Were Law and Necessity about to square off? Justin wondered when he saw an Oakland police car pull into the Goodwill Industries parking lot. It parked right in the middle of the lot, facing the old Ward's building and its needy new occupants. A wave of uneasiness traveled up and down the rope of brown men, but soon they went back to their favored postures. Justin surmised the workers were accustomed to being watched by the law.

He glanced at the cops. At the moment, the officers were more interested in the contents of their Taco El Grullense's meal containers. Any confrontation with the brown men at the Ward's building would have to wait till after breakfast. Too bad. He found himself thinking how welcomed a chase would be at that moment. The thought tickled his conscience, and he smiled at his own contradictions. Gloria would chuckle at that one, too.

A man passing by Justin's van caught his interest. He was also the center of attention for two women volunteers at the Goodwill thrift store. The ladies ran to the window and waved at the man, who greeted them by stretching out his arms towards them. The women covered their coy delight with hands over their mouths. The man turned in a circle, slowly, as if to model his outfit for them—black denim jacket and pants, black western shirt and bolo tie, a black hat, and a pair of black-and-white cow's hair boots. He took off his hat and bowed before them. Then, he strutted to the end of the parking lot and jay-walked across the street to Ward's. He greeted two of the day laborers with a handshake.

What was Fermín Castro's line of work? Dressed like that, surely not a day laborer, Justin concluded as he got out of his van and walked across the street.

"Fermín Castro?" Justin asked.

The two men Fermín had been talking to stepped back. Fermín looked at Justin and answered his query with a head nod. Justin handed him Joe Mendoza's note. Fermín read it and said, "*Sí. Dígame.*"

"At Vista Point, did you see a black man—*un señor negro?*"

"No black man. *Ningún señor negro. Sólo una señorita, muy bonita.*"

A dozen questions and answers later, half in English and half in Spanish, Justin ascertained that Fermín had seen another woman, in addition to Ramona, parking down the road to Vista Point. The other woman was young and dressed in black sweats, her head wrapped in a black knitted cap. She'd gotten out of her metallic blue, brand-new Mustang. When Fermín saw her, he slowed down.

"What made you suspect her?" Justin asked.

"No. *No la sospeché. La admiré. La verda'*, I like ladies. But she too skinny, no woman I really like. She looks me. Pretty eyes, but . . . *desdeñosos.*"

"*¿Cómo?* What do you mean?"

"Very . . . *arrogantes*, you know? She says me, Wat you looking at, fock'r. *En la mano,* she has keys ring with a l'il, l'il doll. You know? L'il girls like."

"A Barbie doll?"

"Yes. Borbee and a *tubito.*"

"A tube. A container?"

"Yes. Small, red an' jellow. She points me wid it. Am not sure wat." Fermín gestured as if he were holding an aerosol container and spraying in the air.

"Pepper—chile—spray?"

"Yes. I go. She go too."

"To Vista Point?"

"Yes. Good I say you?"

"Very good." Justin reached in his wallet and took a couple of twenties out.

Fermín refused the money. "No need. I got job. Pay okay."

Justin went back to his van and sat in it, mulling over the new information. The woman described by the substitute messenger was much younger than Elizabeth or Muriel Ozuna. Oz had not been anywhere near Vista Point. He snuck a look at the brown Dodge van still parked in the lot next to the furniture store. Who was Oz? And the woman? Still two big question marks in the puzzle. He reached for his cell phone and called his friend Tito. Tito informed him he had not been able to obtain a name or address for the key, but he was sure it was a safe key. He had found an old Masterlock equipment catalogue. Justin was welcome to come to his house and take a look at a picture of the safe in question. Justin agreed to meet him later that afternoon.

A subsequent call to Elizabeth clarified the identity of the man watching the Saucedo's home.

"The man is a reporter for *The Oakland Guardian*. I talked to him. He was waiting for me when I arrived home this morning. Mr. and Mrs. Serna are on their way here from Gilroy. I'm expecting them any minute."

"What did the *Guardian* reporter want?"

"He wanted my opinion about a very controversial military high school, a charter school, Mayor Jerry Brown's pet project. You know Jerry favors charter schools. He wants more control over the school district and has taken on the Board of Education and the teachers' union. I told the reporter I oppose government-subsidized charter schools. The city and state need to put more money into Oakland's public schools. At any rate, this man is a bona fide reporter. But, listen, I've got to go. The Sernas just arrived."

Dead end. Justin turned his phone off and started his van. He moved slowly across the Goodwill Industries parking lot, keeping an eye on the brown Dodge van, which also began to back out of its parking spot, heading for the exit. Facing each other across the intersection, the two vehicles waited for the green light. Justin turned his left blinker on and inched to the middle of the intersection. Oz's van stood in place. Justin made the turn and Oz followed him at a reasonable distance.

What did Oz hope to accomplish by following him? It had something to do with the key to the safe, with the safe itself, perhaps. But what?

Justin headed home. He checked his messages and called Gloria in Lake Tahoe. He talked to her briefly about the case, but did not mention Oz or the fact that his van was bugged and he was being followed. Why worry her? She deserved her rest. He looked out his office window. Oz's van was parked across the street, in plain sight.

He spent the afternoon working in his wood shop. As he got ready to leave for his friend Tito's house, he checked the action outside. Oz had probably gotten tired or hungry and had left. He strapped his holster and gun on, picked up an extra ammunition clip, and headed out, looking forward to a cold glass of his friend's home brew, good conversation, and a look at the picture of the elusive safe, where someone's secrets and the answers to his many questions lay in store.

TWELVE
Intruder on Harbor View

AS SOON AS DORA SAW LIGHT in Beatrice's window, she called her. Wasting no time, she asked Beatrice if she could arrange with Vincent's landlord to let her into his apartment.

"No need for that. I have a key to his apartment," Beatrice said, then fired a round of questions and comments: "What do you expect we're going to find there? Information about the man in the photo? I already went through his apartment. I couldn't find anything, not a safe. Even if we find it there, I don't have the combination. He didn't leave it for me. I did find a paper with numbers written on it, but . . . I don't know anything about safe combinations. Do you?"

"Hush, hush. Slow down. Why don't you get a sweater and meet me in five minutes. My car. You know where I park."

Dora put on a jacket. She toyed with the idea of taking her gun but decided the search of an apartment hardly called for that kind of protection.

A half hour later, the soft glow of a Tiffany lamp on a timer welcomed Dora and Beatrice to Vincent's apartment on the ground floor of a four-unit apartment house on Harbor View.

Dora turned her attention to the task at hand immediately. She let her eyes guide her to any unusual or out of place items in the front room. A leather sofa and matching easy chair, end tables with twin lamps on them, metal-framed prints on the wall—everything seemed to fit together well. There were no boxes on tables, no furniture with drawers in it. Dora checked the locks on the living room windows before walking into the kitchen.

Beatrice was sure she had seen what could well be the safe combination written on an index card in a kitchen drawer. Dora checked the drawers in the kitchen. Her search yielded nothing but unpaid bills and a mug shot of Vincent. It looked like a passport photo. She prayed Vincent had not decided to leave the country. She did not have enough miles with United for a trip abroad. The photo of Vincent that Beatrice had supplied her was not as detailed as the mug shot in the drawer, so she put it in her jacket pocket. She checked the numbers on an index card. Most likely a credit card number, she decided.

Beatrice insisted on going through every cabinet and cupboard, while Dora made sure that the kitchen windows and door were locked.

"Does your brother always keep things so neat and organized?"

"I'm the manic, but he's the compulsive. He certainly tops all my obsessions. Runs in the family," Beatrice said and laughed. "I think that's why it takes him a long time to finish a story. I tell him—imagine me saying this—I tell him that he has to be humble enough to do the best he can and let the story go at some point. Persnickety. That's Vincent."

"He's fastidious, all right. A real run-of-the-mill perfectionist," Dora said facetiously.

Beatrice laughed aloud, then covered her mouth to muffle her laughter. "The neighbors," she explained when she saw Dora's amused look.

The timer clicked the lamp in the living room off. Beatrice reached for the switch next to the connecting door between the kitchen and living room and turned the light off before she and Dora headed for the bedroom.

Dora walked into the bedroom and immediately turned her attention to the objects on a computer table and desk. A PC, monitor, and printer. A phone receiver connected to a FAX-phone-answering machine were both unplugged. She plugged both in to check on previous messages. They had all been erased. Vincent had obviously wanted or expected no one to reach him. She unplugged them.

Neatly stacked in a plastic tray was a ream of lavender typing paper.

"First draft of each chapter in longhand; first typed draft on lavender paper; final draft on blue paper," Beatrice remarked on her brother's writing idiosyncrasies.

Dora acknowledged her client's explanation with a nod as she opened the first of two drawers in a utility cabinet. In the top drawer, a large tray displayed an assortment of clips, tacks, soft and hard erasers, staples and other office supplies, and reams of computer paper. The bottom drawer contained a stack of stenographer books. Only one of them had been used. It had the initials R.M.S. on the cover and was dated December, 1999. Dora pulled it out and put it in her handbag to look at later. Strange, Dora thought, no personal files, no folders with even a phone bill in them. Most likely, his personal documents were in the safe they were looking for.

She turned the computer and monitor on. "If he was typing up the first draft, it must still be here. Maybe he made a back-up file," she told Beatrice.

"I'm afraid not. Knowing him, he probably had it on a disk. That way, he could carry it with him."

"Let's check, anyway."

Before Dora had a chance to ask her client if she knew her brother's password, Beatrice, annoyed, said, "I just told you. He takes the disk everywhere with him. Don't you believe me?"

Dora tried to remain calm as she answered, "I do. But you are not trained as an investigator. No one would expect you to know what to look for." She looked at her client.

Her explanation seemed to satisfy Beatrice, who said, "VC1948."

Dora typed up the password. Beatrice left the room, still upset.

A moment later, Dora was roaming through the writer's body of work—essays, articles, and a long novel, but not the one she hoped to find. Going back to the Windows programs, she began systematically to check every directory or file that could contain the manuscript. She opened a directory that contained a number of interviews with only initials atop each file. One in particular, "RMS," caught her eye. She remembered seeing those initials on the steno book and retrieved it from her handbag. She found a blank disk and copied the material for later review. She had just pulled the disk out and put it in her handbag when a visibly disturbed Beatrice came back in the room.

"There is someone looking in the living room window," Beatrice warned, tugging at Dora's jacket sleeve.

"A neighbor?"

"I don't know."

Dora turned the desk lamp off. She told Beatrice to hide under the desk and stay there. She handed Beatrice her cell phone. If anything happened, she should call nine-one-one, then make a run for the front door and a neighbor's apartment.

Beatrice dropped to the floor and crawled under the desk. She saw a small black notebook on the carpet, reached for it, and put it in her pants pocket.

Dora moved slowly down the hallway, then went into the dark living room, careful not to trip on the furniture. She checked every window there, then headed for the kitchen and breakfast nook. Her eyes scanned the dimly lighted yard and small patio and the area at the foot of the hill in back of Vincent's apartment. The light-colored silhouette moving back and forth along the fence turned out to be nothing more than a windsock tickled by a night breeze. Nothing else stirred out there.

Dora had begun to relax when she heard a noise just outside the kitchen door. She slid open a kitchen drawer and pulled out a knife she had seen in it earlier. Treading softly, she reached the back door and put her ear to the wood. Someone was definitely on the other side of the door, trying to pick the lock. A chilling arpeggio ran up her spine to the nape of her neck, then along her hairline to the joints on each side of her clenched jaw.

When she had first checked the door, she'd noticed how unreliable the lock was. She cupped her hand over the doorknob. It moved inside her hand. She quickly let go of it. She held her breath and waited for the burglar to step in. Nothing happened. She breathed again. She heard creaking and grating noises. The intruder was just outside the door. She moved to a more strategic position and turned the knob button to unlock the door.

The intruder pushed the door open and stepped through the threshold into the dark kitchen. The silhouette of the man was shorter and smaller than Dora had expected.

She was not sure he had a weapon, but she still had the element of surprise in her favor. She lunged towards him, grabbed him by the arm with her free hand and swung him around. He reeled back. She shoved him against the counter, then moved quickly to the door and switched the light on.

Funny business, she thought. A burglar without a gun or knife. Nowadays. But she did not relax. He could still have a gun underneath his oversized sweat suit. He wore a black ski mask over his head and face.

"Hands up where I can see them," she commanded, speaking through her teeth. She did not want Beatrice to hear the goings-on, panic, and do something that would put all of them in harm's way.

The intruder hiccuped twice as he looked at the knife in Dora's hand. His eyes moved left to right rapidly, looking for an avenue of escape. He took a couple of steps. Dora moved to block him. "Don't even think about it," she warned.

He began to wave his arms and hands in the air, like a hysterical scarecrow.

This guy had amateur written all over him. Perhaps a kid breaking into a house for the first time.

"This ain't a toy, you idiot. I know exactly what to do with it. You'd better stop all this nonsense," she told him.

The intruder stopped gesturing in the air and lowered his arms.

"C'mon. Take off the mask." She waved the knife in the air.

The man raised his hands slowly, then stopped. He looked in the direction of the hall. Dora heard a noise. Beatrice, she thought, and began to move towards the hall door, but not fast enough. Beatrice ran into the kitchen but stopped dead in her tracks just inside the door. The man darted towards Beatrice, pushed her aside, then sprinted through the door to the living room. Beatrice reeled back. She tried to steady herself by grabbing onto Dora's arm. Dora helped her up, then rushed out after the man.

The intruder was not familiar with the layout of the living room and tripped on the easy chair. Dora grabbed the edge of his sweatshirt. He kept twisting and jerking, trying to get away. She was losing her grip on the sweatshirt. She threw the knife aside to grab onto him with both her hands. The man reached in his pants pocket and quickly turned around. Dora saw the small tube in his hand. Before she knew it, he pointed it at her and sprayed her face. She felt a stinging sensation around her eyes.

"Pepper spray. Damn!" She raised one hand trying to wipe the spray off her face while she tried to hang on to the man's sweatshirt with the other.

"Leave her alone, you . . . you brute!" Beatrice said as she searched for the wall switch and turned on the ceiling light.

The light pierced Dora's eyes, already irritated by the spray. She tried not to close her eyes, but she had to. She fell to her knees, pulling the man down with her. He struggled hard to free himself from her grip. She felt the man's sweatshirt begin to slip off and hung on to it tighter. Suddenly, the man stopped pulling away, but she could still feel him moving. She soon realized that he was trying to slide out of the sweatshirt. She tried to jerk him around. A little too late. The man had already freed himself. Dora felt a hard blow on her head. She let go of the sweatshirt. She grasped in the air, trying blindly to seize his arm.

"Who do you think you are, coming into my brother's house to steal!" Beatrice kept saying, closer to them now.

Dora felt a gust of air around her right ear, followed by a slap. She surmised that Beatrice had struck the intruder or the other way around. Something snapped, like a rubber band. She felt a second stream of droplets descend on her head, and then heard the front door slam against the wall stopper. Beatrice sneezed.

"What . . . in heaven's name is . . . going on? Come back here!" Beatrice yelled.

"What? What's going on?" Dora said as she tried to open her eyes.

"A bra!" Beatrice replied, coming closer and helping Dora up.

"What? I don't understand!"

"*He* was wearing a *bra*!"

THIRTEEN
The Politics of Sin

DORA HAD BEEN ABLE TO FALL ASLEEP toward morning when the sting of the pepper spray subsided. Bathing her eyes and face in warm water and honey had helped. A solicitous, guilt-ridden Beatrice had stayed with her through the night, assisting in any way she could.

Mid-morning, Dora woke up to the enticing aroma of strong, fresh-brewed coffee and *huevos con chorizo*. These were her comfort smells of childhood, she had once told Beatrice. Beatrice remembered and Dora was grateful. Dora savored every morsel and sip.

"Thanks for driving us home last night, too. I know how much you hate driving at night," Dora said, after breakfast.

Beatrice smiled. Their meal finished, she offered to read to Dora the notes on Vincent's steno pad. They spent an hour deciphering his observations on the character and demeanor of a woman with the initials RMS.

Beatrice put down the notebook as she recapped for Dora. "In a nutshell, RMS is dissatisfied. Willful yet stoic. Loyal to her family even though mother repeatedly tells her she's a whore, a sinner. Father takes mother's side. RMS is foolish enough to believe that her past mistakes will not catch up with her."

Beatrice got up and stretched. "Tess or Eustacia by any other name," she added.

"Who're Tess and Eustacia? What are you talking about?" Dora asked.

"Heroines in Thomas Hardy's novels. He was a British writer. The heroines of his novels are all willful women. All punished for their willfulness," Beatrice explained.

"Boy, you really do know a lot about literature," Dora said, impressed. Beatrice beamed. "But frankly," Dora added, "I prefer historical novels and good police procedurals." When Dora saw Beatrice grin, she asked, "What! You don't like history or mystery?"

"I do. I do."

For a while the two women chatted about their literary preferences. It was a perfect moment, Dora mused. She and her mother had also had moments of camaraderie. But a voice inside Dora warned that her client's mood could change directions as quickly as a fire fanned by gusty wind. She brushed aside her misgivings and enjoyed their conversation.

When there was a lull, Dora said, "Willful or not, this woman writer is the key to Vincent's disappearance."

"Maybe these are the initials of a character's name. Vincent is always jotting down plots, characters, settings," Beatrice suggested.

"Let's find out," Dora said and pulled the computer disk labeled "RMS" out of her handbag. She loaded it into her computer, and she and Beatrice began to read avidly.

One file contained a chronology of events that had taken place at the U.C. Berkeley campus between September 1968 and April 1970. It included detailed notes about strategy meetings among the four minority student groups, and between them and sympathizing U.C. faculty. Other notes were quotes from documents recording the founding of the Third World Liberation Front (TWLF), and the negotiations with the faculty senate, the Berkeley chancellor, and the university-wide administration to fund the development of a Third World College. The college would be dedicated to the study of the four ethnic groups represented by the Third World Liberation Front.

When the U.C. administration failed to fully fund such a college, the TWLF students called for a general strike. Vincent had listed the endless confrontations between students and police, the apathy of the Berkeley and campus communities toward the plight of the minority students, then the deployment of other law enforcement agents to the campus by Ronald Reagan, then governor of California.

A second file contained a more personal account of the experiences and participation of a young woman, purportedly "RMS," in the student strike.

Dora stopped reading for a while. Her eyes were still irritated. Beatrice volunteered to read the rest of the file for her. Dora sat in an armchair, cupped her hands over her eyes, and listened.

Beatrice read: "What do I remember most about February 19, 1969? It was one of the worst, perhaps the worst confrontation ever between the cops and all of us, Third World students. If I close my eyes, right now, I see them all—the sheriff's men, Berkeley and U.C. campus cops, highway patrolmen—lining up on Sproul Plaza and The Avenue. I see their hands, rising then striking us, trying to weaken our determination. I hear the sound of bones breaking, the smell of blood trickling out of broken noses, deep cuts and gashes. I remember how the color of that blood, its odor, stayed in my eyes and nostrils for weeks. But what scared the soul out of me wasn't so much their contempt for us. It was the cops' rage, blind rage that numbed reason and hushed conscience. Our humanity disappears when we cross that line, and we lose all capacity for compassion and love of ourselves and others. We lose respect for life itself. Inflicting pain becomes something natural, killing just a fact of life. Raping . . . raping your enemy's women, leaving your seed in them is the greatest conceivable humiliation, the ultimate victory over your enemy."

Beatrice had been reading at a good pace, but she was beginning to race. She paused to catch her breath, then asked Dora, "Do you recognize this?"

"Uh-huh. Chapter Four," Dora said, referring to Vincent's manuscript.

Beatrice read aloud again:

"There are nights I wake up panting, sweating, screaming. I want to remember now, and yet, dread the memories. But it doesn't matter what I want or fear. No amount of alcohol or *mota* can now stop memory's deluge. . . . He was dating my best friend. Unable to resist him, I had let him kiss me a couple of times, fondle my breasts and ass. Something in me made me resist him. Perhaps it was fear, because I was still a virgin. Age twenty and still a virgin. But I wanted him. There were nights when I lay awake, delirious as if seized by a sudden fever, a captive of my own secret desire for him, a desire as primordial as fire. I wanted him to touch me. I wanted to feel, all of him. I imagined how it would feel to have his mouth suck my nipples, his tongue cut a path down to my clitoris, his hardness in me. I walked through countless sleepless nights so near madness."

"Whew. Good God! I feel hot up above and down below already. This is better than a Harlequin romance . . . not that I've ever read one of those," Beatrice said.

"Would you stop editorializing and read," Dora said, but deep inside she agreed with Beatrice's comments. She had also begun to feel hot "up above and down below."

"I knew the scent of his body. I had smelled it before, when he took me target shooting. He'd hold me from behind and help me aim and shoot. I would recognize that odor, the way he touched me, anywhere, anytime.

"That day, I was sure it was him. I was sure he had dragged me out of the riot and into his car. I had lost consciousness when a cop hit me on the head with his baton. Then suddenly, I regained consciousness only to find a hood covering my head, hands touching my breasts. Even then, I'm ashamed to confess, I remember how excited I was, how I longed to feel him inside me. My mind filled with his scent, anticipating the pleasure already, I opened my legs. I guided his hand down to my crotch. I heard him say something I couldn't quite make out. I remember saying, 'Don't talk. Not now. I want you. Inside me.' Then someone spoke again. It wasn't him. Someone else was there. Then he and another man whispered near me. I couldn't hear what they were saying but they both sounded angry. Far away, it seemed, I could hear the clatter of the battle raging between students and cops. I wasn't supposed to be there, with him. I tried to take the hood off, but someone pinned both my hands above my head. Suddenly my sweater was being pulled above and over my head. My hands were caught in the sleeves. I knew it wasn't him. I knew it was *the other*. Fear inched its way through my mind. The darkness inside that hood became oppressive. I was gasping for air. Then I felt ice-cold fingers pinching my nipples hard, so hard I wanted to scream. I couldn't. He began to pull my clothes off. I remember saying, 'Not like this, please. Wait. I want to see you. Let's go to my place.'

"I kept saying it over and over. To no avail. He was beyond reach. I knew what was coming. I began to fight him. When he raised me and thrust into me, I knew it was over. But I kept struggling to free myself. That made it worse. He began to punch my breasts, my stomach, everywhere. He pushed harder inside me. My head was banging against the door. I couldn't catch my breath. Everything went dark in my head. Next thing I remember, I was being dragged out of the car and kicked. He rolled me over and took off the hood. 'Bitch,' he said.

"I wanted to get up but I couldn't. I didn't dare move. Then I heard the screech of tires, a car speeding away. I don't remember exactly what I did next. Somehow I got my clothes on again. I crawled, then walked. Suddenly I was back on Bancroft Way, near the campus. I saw the flashing lights of an ambulance. I tried to run but fell on my face instead. I dragged myself all the way to the ambulance. I felt someone lifting me and putting me on a stretcher and carrying me into the ambulance. I fainted. I opened my eyes again the next morning in the hospital. I had been raped, a nurse told me. Should she contact the police on my behalf? Did I want to press charges? Back then nurses and doctors were not required to call the police if they suspected rape. It was up to me. All I could think of was what my mother would say if she found out. I said no, no cops. All I could feel was a great sadness at his betrayal. Why had he, this man I loved, let that happen to me? I hated him."

Beatrice stopped reading. She wiped the tears from her eyes with the back of her hand.

"Don't stop now. What happened to her?" Dora asked.

"That's all there is," Beatrice answered. "I don't think I could read the rest, even if there were more. I'm going to be sick."

Beatrice ran to the bathroom. She came back a while later with a box of tissues. She handed one to Dora, and they both proceeded to blow their noses a few times.

"Who is R.M.S.? Is she fiction or flesh and blood?" Dora asked, voicing a mental query.

Beatrice got up abruptly and left the room. "I have to get something from my room," she said. She came back a few minutes later, holding a small black book in her hand.

"What's that?" Dora inquired.

"I'd forgotten I had Vincent's address book. I found it under his desk when you went to the kitchen and got into that fracas with the man-who-was-a-woman," Beatrice explained as she sat down and began to leaf through her brother's address book. Noticing numbers and letters that did not make sense, written by Vincent next to her own name and address, Beatrice showed the entry to Dora. "Could that be the safe combination?" She showed Dora the numbers.

"Indeed it could be, my good Watson," Dora congratulated Beatrice, whose eyes sparkled with delight. "The only problem now is finding the safe. Any luck with the initials?" she asked.

Beatrice leafed through the address book. "Bingo! Two possibilities. Rose Marie Smith and R.M. Serna."

"All right! We're in business," Dora exclaimed. "Let me have Serna's number. I'll call from my cell phone. You call Rose Marie Smith. Use this phone." Dora pointed to the receiver hooked up to her computer.

"What do I say?" Beatrice inquired.

"Identify yourself. Tell her that Vincent's out of town but asked you to call her about the manuscript," Dora suggested.

Beatrice agreed with a head nod and got to the task immediately.

Dora decided to use the same story. She went to the living room and dialed the other number. The phone rang quite a few times. Dora heard the familiar click when a call is transferred to a voice machine. Soon after, a taped woman's voice, possibly R.M. Serna, advised the caller to leave a message. Should she, Dora wondered for an instant, but decided instead to end the call and try the number again later.

Dora could hear Beatrice still talking on the phone, so she pulled the phone book out. Her search for an R.M. Serna and her address was fruitless.

Dora paid more attention to Beatrice's conversation when the latter said, "I'm truly sorry you waited for him so long. I know it was raining. But he was called out of town on business, suddenly. Of course I'll give him your message. Thank . . . thank you. Nice talking with you, too. Good-bye."

Beatrice raised her hands and laced them over her head. She sighed. "Poor Rose Marie. She and Vincent had a date that night he disappeared. At least I fixed things for him if he's still interested," she said. "How about R.M. Serna? Any luck?"

Dora shook her head.

"Where is he? I wish he would get in touch."

Dora patted Beatrice's hand. "He'll turn up. Or we'll find him. So, did you ask Rose Marie about the manuscript?"

"She isn't a writer. She's a secretary at a legal office, knows nothing about any manuscript."

"I'm thinking that if R.M. Serna is a published writer, she must be listed somewhere, like Gloria suggested. Maybe dot-com booksellers." Dora logged on to the Internet and began her search through several booksellers' websites. "Here we go. Ramona M. Serna is the author of two books of poetry. The first is *Paths* and the second, *Circles. The Color of Darkness* is the title of her new collection of personal essays on writing. She teaches literature and creative writing for the Peralta Colleges in Oakland. We've got her," Dora said.

Beatrice reached for the phone book and located the numbers for Laney and Merritt, the two Peralta community colleges in Oakland. She wrote down the human resources number at both colleges and handed the slip to Dora.

"You're doing just fine. Make the calls," Dora said to Beatrice's delight.

While Beatrice was busy tracking down Ramona M. Serna, Dora went into the bathroom to bathe her eyes again. She looked at herself in the mirror. Her brown eyes looked glassy; her cinnamon-colored skin showed patches of darker red around her nose and cheeks. The effects of the pepper spray. She tried to comb her curly auburn hair, but the comb got stuck in it. Her hair was sticking out in all directions, wider than the State of Texas, her mother had once told her. She reached for the brush, sat on the toilet seat cover, and proceeded with the slow task of disentangling her tresses, then pulled it all behind her head with an elastic band.

Dora called Art Bello, who confirmed that Ramona M. Serna was the woman writer she searched for. He and Myra were sure. She thanked him and made a mental note to send him and Myra a bottle each of that nice Meridian Cabernet they liked. She went back to her office to check on Beatrice's progress.

"Of course. I understand. Sorry to hear that." Beatrice sounded like an efficient, competent secretary. "I see. Highland Hospital. Room 1213. Got it. Thank you. I truly appreciate your help."

"What's all that about Highland Hospital? Who were you talking to?"

"The dean's secretary at Laney College. All calls about Ramona M. Serna are rerouted to her. Apparently Ramona had a very bad accident a couple of days ago. She was hiking somewhere around Vista Point up in the hills and fell down a ravine. She nearly broke her neck. She's been in a coma at Highland."

Dora sat down in the armchair and snorted. "This changes everything. If she is the woman we're looking for and she's been in a coma for a couple of days already, then who the hell was that masked woman who broke into Vincent's house last night? And what was she looking for?"

"I can't stand this. We're going nowhere!" Beatrice said exasperated. "I've never been good at puzzles."

"We're not back at square one. But something is missing in this picture, true. What is it? Ramona hires Vincent to write her story. She claims she's been raped by a man with the aid of another man she's in love with. Why does she hire Vincent to write about it, thirty years after the rape, and when she's a perfectly capable writer herself? There isn't much in her account that would be detrimental to anyone's reputation, other than hers. Why make it public now?"

"Maybe she wants people to know about it, but not directly. Maybe now she feels safe revealing who the rapist and his accomplice were," Beatrice speculated.

"Maybe. But then she has to know their identity, or strongly suspects who her attackers were. Could be she has some proof."

"If you had that kind of proof, would you have let them get away with it back then?" Beatrice asked.

"We're talking about something that happened in 1969. Thirty years ago, women, rape victims in particular, were reluctant to go public, let alone prosecute the rapists. Even when prosecutors decided to file criminal charges against rapists, the victims' lives were put under a microscope. Their sexual conduct, even their most intimate thoughts, were used as evidence against them. But . . . what if . . . if these two men were well known? What if they were Chicano students involved in the Chicano civil rights movement at Cal? A political nightmare. Ramona M. Serna wasn't about to walk into that swamp. There was too much at risk," Dora concluded.

"Wait. Too fast for me," Beatrice complained.

"Think about it. News of a rape perpetrated by Chicano student leaders on a co-ed, even if she too was a Chicana, would have nullified the students' demands. The U.C. administration would have seen to that, quickly and efficiently. The public clamor for justice would have backed them up. Ramona M. Serna would have been made into a martyr by the administration and the police, used more effectively than a machine gun to defeat the students' insurrection." Dora paused. "But there's another possibility. What if someone had exactly that in mind?"

"If you're thinking what I think you're thinking, you're mad," Beatrice said. "To think that the U.C. administration would be involved in something so . . . despicable?"

"It isn't as inconceivable as you think. Let's say it was a white student or students who did it. The administration would try to cover it up," Dora said. "But Chicanos . . . Chicanos wouldn't be protected," she added.

"I still can't believe it."

"No? Not only in academia. It happened everywhere, even in the Navy. It was one of my father's greatest disappointments, something he fought against all his life. Prejudice by the white military brass. Their fear was that the 'Afros and the Chinks and the Greasers' would avail themselves of power, power they would use in turn against the military establishment. They made sure many times that minority soldiers fought the wars but never made it above the rank of lieutenant, like my father." Dora paused. "Ramona's rapists had to be pretty sure that they could get away with it. Who could enjoy that kind of certainty?" Dora thought about it for a few seconds. "Of course, the only person who knows the answers is in a hospital bed in critical condition, perhaps silenced forever. Her confession to Vincent was not enough. Her desire to bring them to justice through Vincent's book was nothing more than wishful thinking. If she had any proof to offer, Vincent had it and he has disappeared with it."

Dora's eyes lit up. "But what if . . . ?" She sprang up from her chair as if a bolt from the blue had just hit her.

Not knowing what was going on, Beatrice also rose to her feet. "What if what?"

"Think very carefully. We went over every inch of your brother's apartment, looking for the safe he told you about. He even sent you the key for it. We know the safe is not in his apartment. Does your brother keep things at any other location? Does he have a storage locker somewhere?"

"Not that I know of, unless . . ." Beatrice paused.

"Yes?"

"He rents a garage from a neighbor. But as far as I know he keeps only the car and a few boxes of old clothes, memorabilia, old manuscripts there."

"When was the last time you were there?"

"About two years ago, when we went looking for some of my mother's old Christmas ornaments. He wanted me to have them. He doesn't care for Christmas traditions, but I do. I wanted some of those things he had in there."

"So he may have the safe stored there, out of the way, just in case," Dora said. "Do you still have the key to your brother's garage?"

"I do. He gave me his spare so I could go there and haul away anything I wanted for my tree. He told me to keep it."

"Let's go see what's in Vincent's garage," Dora said. "We're going to need the dolly." She went to the laundry room to retrieve her dolly, wheeled it out and loaded it into her car trunk.

Beatrice joined her on the sidewalk but seemed hesitant to get in the car. Dora prompted her. Beatrice did not move. She looked physically and emotionally spent. She handed Dora her key ring. "My brother's garage is two doors down from his apartment. The blue house with the two redwood trees in front."

Dora took the key ring. "What's the matter? Why aren't you going with me?"

"I'm a coward. But I want to remember him alive. I don't want to see him . . . you know . . . ," Beatrice offered as an apology.

"I understand. I'll call you from there."

The memory of her mother's body as Dora identified her for the sheriff flashed through her mind. For years she had fought against that memory. She wanted so much to remember her mother, even if unloving toward her, alive. Fate had been unkind to her. She would make sure Beatrice was spared the horror.

FOURTEEN
Seagulls at the Sanctuary

OZ WAS BACK EARLY THE NEXT MORNING. Justin took his time getting ready to leave his house. On purpose, he took care of daily errands: to the post office to buy stamps he did not really need, to the offices of lawyers who usually had subpoena work for him and Gloria. Anything and everything to get Oz worked up, annoyed enough to show his hand. Oz stuck to Justin like nail to flesh throughout the boring morning routine. Near eleven, Justin's cell phone rang.

Art Bello greeted him and immediately proceeded to tell him he had just had a long talk with Elizabeth, who had informed him that Justin was looking into Ramona Serna's so-called accident for her.

"I don't know how important this might be, bro', but I think you should have a talk with Dora Saldaña," Art said.

"What's the connection?" Justin asked. Knowing Oz would be listening, he refrained from mentioning Dora's name or repeating anything Art said.

"Dora asked Myra and me to read a manuscript. She's looking for two writers, a man and a woman. The man, her client's brother, is missing. But the other writer, the woman, is Ramona M. Serna. I found some of Ramona's early writings. I thought she had abandoned the project long ago. Apparently, she didn't and asked this other writer, Dora's client's brother, to write the story for her. I thought I'd let you know."

"I'll look into it. Thanks, *carnal*," Justin said.

Quite a twist, he thought as he went into a McDonald's to call Dora from a pay phone there. By now, he thought, Oz would be near the end of his patience. Hunger would bring the cat home. But Oz was still holding out, Justin confirmed as he looked around and saw Oz sitting in his van outside the McDonald's.

"Hi, partner. Wassup?" Dora greeted him.

"The missing-person case you're investigating. Does it have anything to do with a writer by the name of Ramona Serna?"

"How did you know?"

"Art Bello called me and told me."

"Why in hell would he do that?"

"Now. Don't be mad. The reason he called me is that he knows I'm looking into Ramona's accident for a mutual friend. Do you know Ramona's in a coma at Highland?"

"Yes. My client and I just found out. So you think we're working on the same case?"

"Partly. We need to talk, but I'm being tailed. That guy you saw at the Y. My van is bugged, so I'm calling you from a pay phone. I'll call you later and let you know how we can connect."

Dora agreed, then asked, "How come you haven't debugged the van yet?"

"I'm hoping to use it to my advantage at some point. Talk to you later."

Justin drove slowly down Fruitvale Avenue towards the channel that separated Oakland from the island city of Alameda. He racked his brain for a strategic place, solitary enough at that hour to minimize the risk to others. When he saw the bridge, one of three joining Oakland to Alameda, he decided to head for the bay shore at the other end of the small island city. He went across the bridge. Oz followed.

Justin found a parking spot near the Alameda post office and the South Shore shopping center. He got out and began to walk along the shore, towards the wetlands, which had been designated as a bird sanctuary. The area was protected from curious humans and their pets by a chain-link fence. A variety of birds nested in the wetlands and Justin stopped to look at them. Small birds protected their nests as fiercely as the larger birds, especially from the seagulls waiting to pounce upon the eggs for a quick meal. He looked at his watch. It was eleven o'clock. Soon, the number of noon joggers would multiply, complicating matters.

He threw a furtive look around and spotted Oz's brown van pulling to the curb near the post office. Oz got out and walked around his van, pretending to check the tires. With his hands in his jeans pockets, he began to walk on his side of the road in the direction Justin was heading.

Separated by a two-lane road, they walked their parallel course for a while until a change in the terrain made it impossible for both men to continue. Justin decided to walk toward a ten-foot-long wooden ramp overlooking the nesting areas. It was intended to serve as an observation point for bird watchers. A three-foot-tall chain-link fence rose along the sides and front of the walkway to prevent people from gaining access to the sanctuary. Justin saw a group of seagulls below. They had managed to scare away some of the small birds from their nests and were now feasting on blue-spotted brown eggs. The smaller birds would frequently swoop down on the gulls, still trying to frighten them off. Justin walked to the far end, turned around, and waited.

Oz reached the walkway but stopped a few feet from Justin. He took his hands out of his pockets. "No need for that," he said, pointing at the bulk of the gun underneath Justin's jacket. In an attempt to show Justin he had come in peace, he pulled apart both sides of his jacket, took it off, and threw it over his shoulder. He leaned on the low chain-link fence.

Justin was surprised to see the clear outline of ribs and sternum underneath the sweat-drenched T-shirt Oz wore. He looked at the man's face, then in his eyes. He perceived only a blurry trace of some emotion that for lack of a better descriptor Justin identified as fear.

Under scrutiny, Oz's facial expression changed to bravado and he straightened up. He grinned, but still said nothing.

"What do you want?" Justin finally asked.

"What's mine."

"And what'd that be?"

"The safe."

"So that's what this is all about," Justin thought to himself, then said, "You've been following me for a while, so you know I don't have it."

"But you're getting close, right? When you find it, I want it. It's *my* property."

"What's in it?"

Oz laughed. "Do you really expect an answer or are you just jiving me?"

"What's in the safe?" Justin asked again.

"Insurance papers," Oz said, taking a step forward. Justin stood his ground. "Look. I'd love to stay and chat, but I'm running out of time. I've got to get those papers. My kids are the beneficiaries." Oz took another couple of steps toward him.

Justin did not move from the spot but reached in his jacket and put his hand on the butt of his gun. Undeterred, Oz took another step.

"You want your insurance papers, you answer my questions. I'm getting tired of you." Justin snapped his fingers. "C'mon. What kind of insurance? From whom? Gastón Saucedo?"

Oz laughed, then began to cough. His face turned red. He heaved under the strain, trying to control the coughing. He cleared his throat a few times and finally answered with a raspy voice, "From that son-of-a-bitch? No. I could have taken him out any time. Sending his gorilla to do his job for him."

Elizabeth. Had she known all along her husband had already found Oz? Even if she did not, why had Gastón been so interested in finding Oz? The contents of the safe?

"So you've had dealings with Saucedo. When?" Justin asked.

"No concern of yours," Oz snapped.

Justin shrugged. "Suit yourself."

Changing his mind, Oz said, "Long ago, before he married Liz Ortiz, one of his so-called *security* goons came gunning for me. Saucedo wanted to know if I was the father of Liz's two daughters. He got his answer attached to his gorilla's *cojones* at S.F. General."

"Are you Irene's father?" Justin asked, although he did not expect an answer.

"You really don't get it, poor bastard. That's what Liz told Saucedo."

Oz began to cough hard again. This time the violent spell lasted longer. He gasped for breath. Disoriented, he stepped back. He stretched his hands behind him, trying to hold on to the chain-link fence.

Justin rushed toward him, but before he could grab a hold of him, Oz went over the low fence.

The gulls reacted to the intrusion. Flapping their powerful wings around Oz's face, they rose a few feet in the air. The smaller birds joined the frenzy, still trying to protect their now eggless nests from a new intruder. They kept plunging down, hitting their target a few times with their beaks.

Oz cried out. He started to swing his jacket around to scare them away, but he turned suddenly, slipped in the mud, and bumped into the wooden platform, bruising his face. The gulls landed near him. He was coughing so hard his face was turning purple. The gulls took to the air again.

"Stay down. They'll go away," two joggers behind Justin yelled. "Your friend had better get out of there," they advised Justin.

Oz stopped coughing, fell to his knees, and covered his head with his jacket.

Justin stepped over the fence. He lowered himself to the muddy ground as quietly as possible. He crawled until he was close enough to grab Oz's arm. He began tugging Oz towards the edge of the walkway. He pushed him up until Oz could grab onto the fence. The joggers pulled Oz up and over the fence. Justin climbed up onto the walkway. The seagulls walked around tentatively, looking for whatever was left of their egg lunch.

Blood trickled from a deep cut above Oz's left eye. Shallow cuts and bruises showed all over his gaunt face and his hands. Justin offered him his clean handkerchief. Oz took it and wiped blood and sweat off his left brow.

One of the joggers offered Oz a bottle of water. Oz took it, uncapped it, and took a large swig. Justin thanked the two joggers, who went on their way as soon as they felt the two men had everything under control.

"You should have a doctor look at that cut over your eye. It looks nasty. Should have that cough checked, too. I can take you to Highland," Justin suggested. Nothing better than getting Oz to the hospital, where Elizabeth could have a talk with him.

Oz waved Justin's advice off with his hand. He cleared his throat. "Too late for doctors," Oz said. He sat down on the wooden deck. After a brief pause, he added, "You've probably guessed by now, I'm not well. Hell, let's call a spade a spade. I'm a dying man."

Justin did not respond. He acknowledged the confession with a head nod. Sometimes silence was a better ally, Justin thought as he sat down on a spot across from Oz.

"Beaten by birds, tiny ones at that," Oz said, pointing at the bed of feathers left by the birds. "In all my years with the Bureau, I never got hurt. Not once," he added. "I was a fearless son-of-a-bitch. I even used my real name at Berkeley. None wised up. A real bad dude. That, I was." He chuckled softly.

A fed. That explained a lot. Justin kept quiet.

Oz looked at Justin. "I had all kinds of assignments," he continued. "I lived in holes so deep I thought I'd never find my own way out of them. You name 'em. I was even a Black Panther. Believe it or not, I even returned fire when the cops would come gunning for the brothers. I had to. The cops were shooting at me, too. They had no way of knowing I was on their side. Funny, ain't it? I'm really Puerto Rican, but in the eyes of racists, cops or otherwise, I'm black." He shook his head. "I tell you, there were so many undercover cops and feds in the Black Panther organization, we ended up informing on each other." He seemed amused at the memory.

Oz was lost in thought. Then, almost as if talking to himself, he added, "I have no regrets. Call it brainwash, but I really believed I was helping J. Edgar rid the country of subversive elements. I was a *true believer*, a patriot, only on the opposite side of the fence. All those Vietnam vets complained that they came back, minds and bodies all fucked up, to a country that at best disavowed their bravery and at worst denied them the rights to the medical and financial support they were entitled to. We—all of us deep in the urban trenches—were disowned, too. But while it lasted, we were all soldiers in the great army of J. Edgar Hoover, powerful and mighty. So mighty, some of us really believed we had a license to get the job done at any cost. Supplying guns, women, even drugs, you name it."

"From what I read, I think the CIA supplied the drugs. At least in

East Oakland," Justin commented. He wanted Oz engaged in conversation until he could figure out what Oz was driving at.

"Ah, yeah, the big C. If you can't kill their bodies, kill their fucking wills. Yep! Get the job done any way you can. That was a prime directive for all of us."

"But, did they—you all—really succeed? The black community in East Oakland knows no one is going to help them. So they are now cleaning up their neighborhoods. And the Panthers' organization is still alive in many parts of the country," Justin said.

Oz gave Justin an amused look. "If you're talking about ex-Panther-self-proclaimed-journalist-cop-killer-and-righteous-man Mumia Abu-Jamal, and others like him . . . phh. They don't stand a chance. But you're right, the Company and the Bureau had their own agendas for the Panthers, too. If you ask me, they still do. Abu-Jamal will see the last light of day behind bars. Only way he'll get out is feet first. And, one by one, the rest of them will go down. You can make book on that."

Justin offered no comment. Oz sat quietly for a while, too.

Out of the blue, Oz said, "I'm not the father of Elizabeth's daughter." He turned to look at Justin. "Someone else is."

"How can you be so sure? It happened a long time ago."

Oz smirked. "Oh, I'll remember Liz till the end of my very short life. I know I'm not the father. We fucked only twice, because she wanted it that way, and long before she got pregnant. The math doesn't add up."

"So, why do you think she's saying Irene is your daughter?"

In a child's singsong, Oz said, "That's for me to know and you to find out." He snickered, looked away, then added, "You'll have to ask Elizabeth." He got up, looked at his soiled pants, and slapped his legs to get rid of some of the mud, which had begun to dry.

"What's in the safe you're looking for?" Justin asked as he also stood up.

Oz was quiet for a while but did not make an effort to leave. Justin thought he would not get any more straight answers from him. He was surprised when Oz said, "There was a man . . . he was ATF. We worked together at Berkeley during the student strike and in Colorado."

Justin was not sure where the conversation was going or what an Alcohol, Tobacco and Firearms agent had to do with the case at hand. But he wanted Oz to keep talking. Hoping to gain more information, in a casual tone he asked, "Why Colorado?"

"The Crusade for Justice. We went in. There were rumors that Corky Gonzales was buying guns, preparing for a *true revolution.* Fools! Them and the students at Berkeley. Even with guns, they didn't have a chance in hell. Just like the Panthers in Oakland. The Company aside, J. Edgar had his manicured little fingers into everything. For him, the information he had—about anything and everything and everybody—was more powerful than any other weapon, though we were sanctioned to use those, too."

"So why is it important that you find this . . . friend of yours, the ATF?" Justin asked.

"He's no friend of mine. I know where he is. He's now in California's law enforcement, getting a juicy nest egg, ready to run for a seat in the state assembly. He's got some powerful people to back him up. He's in the position to . . . do something for my kids and my wife. When I die—soon enough—I want them to be taken care of. He'll have to do that. Not his choice. But only if I find my safe."

Blackmail, Justin thought. "What's his name and what exactly would he be paying for?"

Oz did not answer, just crossed his arm over his chest and lowered his head. He looked at his muddy shoes, then at Justin. "His name is Patterson. Ron W. Back in the sixties and seventies, he went by the name of Pretty Boy, you know, after the gangster. He had no problem saying that we were the 'good ganstas.'"

"I see. You expect me to relay your message to Pretty Boy. In exchange for what?"

Oz snickered and shrugged his shoulders, but he made no move to leave. Hoping to find out why Oz was telling him about Patterson, Justin asked, "When did you last see him?"

"I haven't seen him in years. Pretty Boy and I were assigned to Denver. We knew the Young Lords had moved part of their operation from New York to Berkeley. They were going to Denver to a youth conference sponsored by Gonzales and the Crusade. We joined the

Young Lords contingent. Many others from all over California were there to attend the conference, too. My wife and kids were supposed to join me in Denver if I had to stay longer. As it turned out, I . . . I was ordered back to the Bay Area after three months."

"Why?" Justin asked. "As you just told me, Corky Gonzales was getting more and more powerful then."

Oz was quiet for a moment. "Truth is, I requested the transfer. Let's just say that I didn't want to . . . keep company with Pretty Boy any longer." He looked at Justin in the eyes and said, "Believe it or not, there were . . . are some things I wouldn't do."

"Such as?"

"Like . . . like taking advantage of women, friends or foes," Oz looked away.

"Rape?" Justin asked, suddenly aware of a possibility he had not considered. His heart sank to his feet as he asked, "Did Patterson rape Elizabeth?"

Oz squinted as if sudden blades of light had pierced his eyes, but he did not answer Justin's question.

"If that's the case, you've got to tell me now," Justin pressed on.

"I want my safe and you're going to get it for me, man. Or you don't get any answers."

Oz had finally put some of his cards on the table. But what if he was bluffing, if there was no truth in what he had just implied about Elizabeth? It could just be a ploy to have Justin do the dirty work. But could he take the chance?

"What's it going to be?" Oz pressed on. "Do we have a deal?"

"When and where did you last see your safe?" Justin asked, trying not to sound as mortified as he felt.

"About two months ago, my place in Oakland was broken into. The back door was pried open. Nothing but the safe was taken. At first I thought my wife—ex-wife—had taken it. She'd filed for divorce. She was always curious about it. But she swears she didn't take it. One thing about Muriel, she's straight as an arrow. Then I thought Saucedo had found out about it and sent one of his goons for it. I still think he did it. I began to keep an eye on him and Liz. But so far I haven't found out where he and Liz stashed it. When they hired you,

I checked you out. You're a P.I. From what I hear, a good one. So I decided to follow you."

Justin said nothing. His mind was racing, trying to fit all the new pieces into the puzzle.

Oz took his silence as refusal. "You think I'm lying. I'm not shitting you. Ask Liz. Ask her. She knows. If she doesn't, that husband of hers knows for sure." Oz took a few steps back. "You have my word. I had nothing to do with what happened in '69. And I am not Irene's father. I want my safe back. I'll get it back any way I have to. Tell her that. I'll be there when you find it. You can make book on that," he shouted, already on his way to his car.

A pair of Canadian geese resting on the ground stretched their wings and took flight as Oz approached them.

Justin watched Oz get in his van and drive down the street. He mulled over the information Oz had provided him. He was now certain that he was not being told everything. Was Gastón Saucedo behind it all? Or had Elizabeth been lying to him and her husband for her own private reasons?

FIFTEEN
A Detective's Daily Bread

DORA FOUND A SPOT ON HARBOR VIEW and parked across the street from the blue house Beatrice had described. She knocked on the owner's door to make him aware of her presence, or she might have the cops all over her, asking questions. When she was certain no one was home, she went back to her car and pulled out a pair of latex gloves and a surgical mask she kept in her trunk. She walked over to the garage. She had just slid her gloves on when her cell phone rang. Beatrice, she assumed, but was surprised to hear Justin's voice instead.

In his usual no-nonsense style, Justin got immediately to the point, asking if they could meet at her house in a couple of hours. She agreed.

She pulled the mask over her mouth and nose and tightened the elastic strap. Just the mere possibility that she would find Vincent there made her heart race and her breathing quicken. What she needed most was air flowing unimpeded into her lungs, but less air was a better prospect than the foul smell of rotting flesh. With a shaking hand, she put the key in the padlock, unlocked it, and removed it.

"On the count of three," she whispered. She grabbed the garage door handle with both hands and pulled it up with all of her might. The garage door gave way with a violent shudder. There was no car in it. No signs of foul play anywhere she could immediately see. No flies. She pulled her mask down and breathed. The odor of mold and stale fumes hung in the still air. She relaxed a little.

The garage contained an assortment of labeled and neatly stacked boxes, some old tote bags and suitcases, an old red toolbox, a futon mattress resting on two small, black, metal trunks. She checked the floor for visible blood stains. There were none. Searching someone's personal belongings, even when that person might be a criminal, always bothered her. Women were supposed to be curious creatures, according to most men. But in circumstances such as these, men availed themselves of the authority to invade anyone's privacy much more quickly. This was for a good cause, she kept telling herself as she searched through boxes and suitcases.

An hour later, all she had left to look into were the two small, black trunks. They were locked, and Dora tried every key Beatrice had given her, but none fit. She went back to her car and retrieved her locksmith box—her burglary kit, as she called it. Over the years, she had collected an assortment of handmade tools, skeleton and flat keys, and even trivial items such as diamond nail files. She chose the items she thought would help her unlock the trunks and went back to the garage.

She turned the trunks over on their sides and got to the task at hand. It was her lucky day, she thought when one of the flat keys went in and turned in the locks. But she still couldn't open the trunks. She got a screwdriver from Vincent's red toolbox. After a few "damns" and copious sweat to help her effort on, she busted the locks and opened the trunks. She felt a sting in one of her fingers. The edge of the screwdriver had torn the glove and dug into the skin of her middle right finger. "Great," she said under her breath, "not only am I tampering with possible evidence in a crime scene but also leaving my bloody fingerprints all over it."

She opened the first trunk. Neatly tucked inside it was the safe she and Beatrice had desperately been looking for. She had not brought the safe key or combination, so she decided to take the safe with her. Now she was removing evidence. But it was too late for all those considerations. She quickly looked through the contents of the other trunk. It contained mostly manuscripts and old correspondence.

Lifting the safe onto the hand truck took quite a bit of effort, but loading it into her car trunk left her gasping for breath. At least all that sweat bathing her eyes had washed away any remaining trace of the pepper spray.

She called Beatrice to let her know she had found the safe, and, fortunately in this case, no traces of Vincent.

Dora had to admit she felt excited at the prospect of reviewing the contents of the safe. A lot of secrets, she hoped, judging merely by its weight. And secrets were a P.I.'s daily bread. Just like a man, she realized and chuckled at her contradictions.

Half an hour later, she and Beatrice were staring at a wad of one-hundred-dollar bills in an envelope, the first thing they'd pulled out of the safe.

"Where on earth did Vincent get this much money? There must be at least two thousand dollars here," Beatrice said, counting the bills. She looked at Dora and asked, "Could this be what that thief, that woman, was looking for in his apartment?"

"Hard to tell. Let's see what else is in it."

They proceeded to take out several thick folders tied with a string and a notebook with the initials "OZ."

"I wonder what OZ means?" Dora asked.

"A mythical land?"

"I doubt we'll be reading about Dorothy and the Cowardly Lion," Dora said.

Beatrice opened the notebook and skimmed through it. "This is some sort of log, maybe a journal."

Dora untied the folders. Each folder had the FBI seal on its cover and a year written on its tab.

"Wow! Where did your brother get his hands on all these uncensored FBI files? They date back to 1968 and up to 1975." Dora picked out the folder marked 1969 and began to read, with Beatrice looking over her shoulder.

"Oz was a federal agent, as far as I can tell. What he has to do with your brother, I can't say yet." She kept reading.

The doorbell rang a while later. Dora looked out the front window. Justin was standing at the front door. She told Beatrice to stay in her office while she went to let him in.

Dora was surprised to see Justin so unkempt. His hair, shirt, pants, and shoes were full of mud. By no means was Justin the epitome of male elegance, but he was usually a neat, if casual, dresser. What mess had he gotten into?

Justin read the question in her eyes and said, "I had to rescue someone. Over there." He pointed to some indistinct place with his right hand. "I'd better take my shoes off."

Socks on, he'd barely stepped into the house when he and Dora heard a scream.

"Beatrice," she said and ran to her office, followed by Justin close behind.

Beatrice was saying, "Oh, my God! She was telling the truth. Look at these women. They were all raped! How many more? How many more?"

"Get a hold of yourself." Dora knelt down to comfort her.

Justin stopped at the door, his eyes fixed on the safe and on Beatrice, who was kneeling next to it, clutching an open notebook and rocking back and forth. His heart somersaulted in his chest when he saw "OZ" written on the cover of the notebook. In a matter of seconds, it was pounding furiously against his rib cage.

Dora took the notebook from Beatrice and read the entry on the open page. She turned to Justin and said, "Ramona M. Serna is not among them. These women were raped by an Alcohol, Tobacco and Firearms agent. A busy rapist." Dora paused. Justin's face had gone from red to pale. "Are you okay? You look like you've seen a ghost."

Justin cleared his throat, then answered, "In a way, he—Oz—is a ghost. He's dying."

"Is this Oz the man following you? The man I saw at the Y watching you?"

Justin nodded. He looked at Beatrice, then at Dora. "Could I talk to you alone?" he asked Dora, extending his hand toward the office door.

Dora realized she had not introduced Beatrice to Justin. She quickly made amends. Justin shook Beatrice's extended hand and helped her up.

"Beatrice's brother Vincent is missing. He's a writer, apparently commissioned by Ramona M. Serna to write her story."

Justin said nothing. Dora called Beatrice to the side and asked if she would mind leaving them alone for a while. She would be in touch later. Beatrice took Dora's request calmly, excused herself, and walked out.

Justin waited until he heard the front door close. "I don't think it's a good idea to have your client involved further. No way to tell what Oz is capable of doing to get his hands on his safe. Patterson, the ATF guy, is a criminal with political aspirations. Not a happy camper when he finds out about the contents of Oz's safe. Anyone we come in contact with from now on is in danger."

Justin filled Dora in on Ramona Serna's accident, which was looking more and more like foul play. He mentioned what Fermín Castro, the substitute messenger, had told him about the young woman in the black sweats and ski cap he saw near Vista Point. His encounter with Willie Oz had added a few answers to the puzzle. Not enough. Now there was the possibility that Elizabeth might have also been raped by Patterson. It explained why he had the feeling that the Saucedos had not been quite so straightforward with him.

"That young woman at Vista Point has got to be the same one that broke into Vincent's apartment," Dora said.

Justin's inquisitive look reminded Dora she had not told him anything about her investigation. She recapped her findings for him. She showed him Jesse Latour's photos, and told him about her suspicion that he was somehow involved in Vincent's disappearance. She had the feeling that Oz's files would shed some light on all the goings-on.

"There's only one way to find out if Elizabeth was also one of Patterson's rape victims. C'mon, we have a lot to read." Dora pointed to the armchair. "Make yourself comfortable." She handed Oz's journal to Justin. She picked up the stack of FBI files and continued reading.

"Look at these photos and bios," Justin told her an hour later. "Oz claims these women were raped by Pretty Boy Patterson. He suspects the count was higher." He got up and laid the open journal on Dora's desk.

"Were Ramona Serna or Elizabeth Saucedo among them?" Dora asked as she got up and moved closer.

"There's no indication. Not here, anyway. But Oz claims the count was higher. For some reason, he omits the names of the other victims. He mentions only these three women in Denver. He also has photos, showing who I think is Patterson, beating and shoving the women into unmarked cars."

Dora looked at the photos. "I don't understand. Why is Ramona

Serna not among them? How about her claim that she was also raped by a man, who could well be Patterson, perhaps aided by Oz? Listen to this." She read excerpts from Ramona's account of her own rape.

"It might be that Oz was there. He knew what Patterson was going to do and he let it happen. An accomplice. He wouldn't write about it—self-incriminating. But all these women lived in Denver. From what you and Oz told me, there might be a connection with that Denver man you mentioned."

"Possibly," Dora said and looked again at Patterson's alleged rape victims in Denver. Each victim's first name was printed under her respective photo. The first young woman was either a black Latina or African American by the name of Sheila. Twenty-three years old, she had been a beginning teacher at West High in Denver. The second, a fair-skinned, light-brown-haired woman by the name of Felicia was twenty-one years of age, a Chilean foreign student at Boulder. She had been doing some tutoring at the Crusade for Justice's Escuela Tlatelolco for a few months. The third woman, Elena, was seventeen and a student at West High. She had been very active in the students' school boycotts and had worked closely with the leaders of the Crusade's youth movement in Colorado.

"That bastard," Dora said, "he's going to have to pay for all he did."

"Bringing Patterson to justice for what he did so long ago is not our concern right now. The man is a heartless criminal with a badge, no question about it. But, for obvious reasons, I advise against even getting in touch with him for the time being. We'll see what can be done later," Justin warned. "What's in the files?"

"A lot of stuff having to do with the Crusade for Justice and Corky Gonzales's activities in Denver, especially about the Chicano youth movement. Did you participate in any of the youth conferences sponsored by the Crusade?"

"No. I didn't. But Gloria attended a couple of them. Ask her. Also, you might want to ask Luis Móntez. He was involved, too."

"By the way, thanks for the reference. Luis was the one who sent me Jesse Latour's photos."

"You're welcome. You can trust Luis."

"I'm going to make copies of all these papers and the journal, just in case. I'll make a copy for you. What do we do with the originals and the safe?" Dora asked.

"It's better if you keep the safe and its contents here. Oz doesn't know about you. And I'll make sure he doesn't find out where you live."

"There's something still bothering me," Dora remarked. "Vincent ends up with Oz's safe. From what he told you, Oz says someone broke into his house and stole it about two months ago. He suspects the Saucedos are behind the theft. If that's the case, they must also know about Vincent. The only link among them is Ramona Serna. Could she have stolen Oz's safe? Maybe she gave it to Elizabeth to keep for her. With Ramona in a coma in the hospital, Elizabeth might be the woman who broke into Vincent's house to retrieve it."

"But why would Elizabeth do that? There's nothing implicating her in any wrongdoing, not even the mention of her name anywhere in Oz's journal. Besides, the woman Fermín Castro saw at Vista Point was young."

"So that's that?"

"Not quite. I do think the Saucedos know more than they're telling. I intend to find out what that is. Right now." Justin closed the journal and handed it to Dora. He got ready to leave.

"How do I get the copies of this material to you?"

"I'll call you when I get back to my office and tell you when to do it. Here's the key to my office." Justin took out two keys from his ring. "The other key is to my flat downstairs. You know the layout. I'll distract Oz. Then, if you don't mind, drop the copies at my office."

"How are you going to get back into your house?"

"No trouble. I keep spares in my van. Wait for my call."

Dora accompanied him to the door. She was suddenly in need of reassurance. She headed for the locked kitchen drawer, where she kept her father's gun.

SIXTEEN
Sins of a Daughter

JUSTIN ARRIVED AT HIGHLAND HOSPITAL as the sun's large golden disk had begun its descent into the misty Pacific. He saw Oz in his van, parking down the street. He hoped to have a word with Elizabeth at the hospital rather than at her home, where nothing would escape Gastón's scrutiny. He was not in luck as Elizabeth had left ten minutes before he arrived. But Mr. and Mrs. Serna were still there, the ICU nurse told him. Justin felt obligated to see them.

George Serna was an affable man, even under these sad circumstances. His wife Lena, on the other hand, was an austere woman, with a stern, heavily accented voice. Immediately upon meeting Justin, she began to complain about her daughter's lifestyle: a din about the repeated occasions her daughter had offended, insulted, or humiliated her.

"My daughter, she's committed the worst sin a woman can commit. Now God has punished her for her sins. Life is sacrosanct and only God can give it or take it."

Justin wanted to ask what a woman's worst sin was, but Lena Serna gave him no chance to wedge a word in. George Serna, obviously embarrassed by his wife's behavior, kept quiet throughout her dark litany, glancing at Justin every so often with apologetic eyes.

Justin expressed his regret about Ramona's condition and got away as soon as he could. Oz was still there and drove a short distance behind him all the way to Elizabeth's house. But Justin couldn't care less what the old fed was up to at that point. They would face each other again when Justin was ready for it.

Justin kept pondering Mrs. Serna's last comment about the worst sin a woman could commit, a sin so great God would have a need to inflict severe punishment on the female perpetrator.

He had been raised Catholic. So had Ramona and Elizabeth. Tempting men, especially a married man or a priest, having sex out of wedlock, and aborting a pregnancy were among Catholic women's major offenses. Less serious sins included swearing, dressing provocatively, and drinking, or challenging parents' or husbands' authority. As he was growing up, he had heard them all cited among the many taboos for Mexican Catholic women of Mrs. Serna's generation. Which of those was Ramona's worst offense?

By the time he rang the bell at Elizabeth's residence, Justin had concluded that Ramona M. Serna had not only been raped, but also gotten pregnant and aborted the fetus. Nothing in that situation merited hell's fire or eternal damnation, for Ramona was the victim, not the perpetrator. But Mrs. Serna had stressed the fact that only God had the right to give or end life. Getting rid of an unwanted pregnancy, even when raped, was in the eyes of the Catholic Church as grave an offense as murder-in-the-first.

He remembered what Art had once told him about Ramona and Elizabeth when he met them back in 1969. Ramona had dropped out of the scene for quite some time then. She had kept in touch only with Elizabeth, her best friend, who some time later had also disappeared for a few months. Only Ramona had not come back with a baby, whereas Elizabeth had. Justin heaved a sigh. Life was indeed full of surprises.

At Elizabeth's house, he parked behind a metallic blue Mustang. He looked around for Gastón's security men, but they were nowhere to be seen. He did not see Elizabeth's BMW, but someone was home. Loud music blared from a stereo somewhere in the house, making the walls and even the front door reverberate. He rang the bell repeatedly. He was getting into his car when he heard the music stop. He rang the bell again. This time, Elizabeth answered the door. She showed him in.

A large painting by Juana Alicia, a San Francisco artist, was on the wall opposite the front door. Justin had admired that particular painting on his first visit to the house. But his delight at seeing it again was now overshadowed by anxiety. He turned his attention to Elizabeth. She was retrieving a small packet of tissues from her handbag, which lay on a chair next to a marble-top table at the entrance. She had just finished eating a sandwich, she explained as she wiped her lips and hands with the tissue.

"I'm going to call Gastón. He said he wanted to hear your report."

"I'd rather you didn't. I want to talk to you first," he said. He took his cell phone out and turned it off.

Elizabeth glanced at him, an obvious question in her eyes. But Justin was now looking intently at the items on the table. Among the key rings on the marble-top table, he saw one with two keys, a tiny Barbie doll and a yellow-and-red pepper spray tube hanging from it. His voice froze in his throat. Life was not finished with its surprises. How was he going to tell Elizabeth that her younger daughter had been seen in the vicinity of Vista Point at the time of Ramona Serna's accident? He cleared his throat but said nothing.

Elizabeth put the tissue packet in her bag and signaled for him to follow her to the kitchen. She offered him a beer, but he declined.

A young woman, who he surmised was Elizabeth's youngest daughter Serena, was in the kitchen, pulling a soda out of the refrigerator. Justin had not met her before. The day of the party, Serena had been spending the night at a friend's house, Elizabeth had told him.

Elizabeth made the introductions. The young woman did not utter a sound. She looked Justin over and smirked, then took a swig of the soda.

With a great deal of makeup on, Serena looked older than seventeen, her age according to Elizabeth. He looked at her arched brows and strikingly beautiful eyes. The look of disdain in them confirmed what Fermín had said about the woman jogger he had seen near Vista Point.

Out of the blue, Serena asked him, "Are you Mommy's new lover?" She kept her eyes fixed on her mother all the while.

Justin realized the question was intended to shock him but most of all to mortify her mother. She had succeeded.

"Serena! Apologize to him. Right now!"

Serena arched her brows and shrugged her shoulders. "He's nothing to me. Why should I?"

A brief mother-daughter argument ensued. But Justin's mind was occupied with all sorts of questions and their dreaded probable answers. Was Serena also the young woman who had broken into Vincent Constantino's apartment? Did she know about Oz's safe? Was she looking for it? Was she doing all that to please her father? Obviously not to please her mother, for whom she seemed to have nothing but animosity.

Serena stormed out of the kitchen. Elizabeth sighed and apologized for her daughter's behavior. Justin saw how tired and distraught she was. Sympathy for her tugged at his heart. What he had to say to her wasn't going to be pleasant. He looked in the direction of the living room as a shadow moved into his peripheral vision, then out of it. Serena was eavesdropping, he guessed. It was going to be difficult to speak honestly with Elizabeth with the young woman close by.

"Can we go outside and talk?" he said, pointing to the patio visible through the sliding door.

She acquiesced with a nod and led him through the family room to the patio. Justin stepped out and onto the patio ahead of Elizabeth, who slid the door closed behind her. Not knowing where to begin, he was quiet for a moment.

Alerted to unpleasant news, Elizabeth asked, "All right. We're alone now. What's going on?"

"Willie Oz has been on my tail for days. I let him catch up to me earlier this afternoon. We had a long talk. He swears he's not Irene's father. I believe him."

Disbelief ran through her eyes. It was soon replaced by anger. "You believe him. I see. Well, then there's no need to trouble yourself any further, is there?" Her furious look belied her contained tone of voice. "Just tell me where we can find him and Gastón and I will take it from there. Send us your bill," she added and began to walk towards the sliding door.

"You won't have any trouble finding Oz. You'll find him right behind me." Justin decided not to tell her that all she had to do was to step outside and have a chat with Oz herself, but not before he got the answers he was searching for. He continued, "Oz won't stop until he's satisfied I don't have what he wants." He took a step towards Elizabeth. "You and your husband have been keeping things from me.

You've made it not only difficult for me to get at the truth, but you've also put me unnecessarily in harm's way. And now you dismiss me as if I were an unwelcome nuisance. If nothing else, we owe each other the truth. And you're going to tell me all there is to know right now," Justin announced in a huff.

Elizabeth turned around and looked at him, trying to gauge his determination. She had never seen him so defiant toward her. In fact, she thought, during the many years they had known each other, he had never gotten angry at her, nor raised his voice to her as he was doing now.

"You haven't been telling me the truth, either," she said in a softer tone.

Also lowering his voice, Justin replied, "I refuse to tell half-truths, if that's what you mean. I don't report to my clients what's happening until I'm certain I have the facts, not rumors nor innuendo. That's why I'm here now."

Accepting the inevitability of the confrontation she knew was about to follow, she sat down on a patio chair. "What is it you want to know?"

"Did you know your husband had you investigated before he married you, that he knew Oz wasn't Irene's father?"

Confusion darkened her eyes. It swiftly turned to pain. She rose to her feet. "I cannot believe he did that. Have me investigated?" she said after a while. Looking at him directly, she continued, "I had already told him all there was about me, the men in my life . . . he knew about . . . you, too."

"I wish I knew why your husband did that. But that's something you'll have to take up with him. But what concerns me is that he already knew Willie Oz wasn't Irene's father, even before he married you. Was it your idea or his to hire a P.I.—me—to find Oz again?"

"It was his idea to hire a detective, but mine to hire you. I told you the truth. We need to find Irene's father. My granddaughter's life depends on getting a bone marrow transplant. Time is running out."

"Who is Irene's biological father?"

"I don't know." Elizabeth straightened up. "Not for sure. . . . I might as well tell you now. Knowing you, you won't desist until you find out. I adopted Irene when she was a newborn baby. I'm not sure who the biological father is. You've got to believe me."

"I gathered as much. Irene is Ramona Serna's biological child, isn't she?" he asked bluntly.

A gust of air rushed out of Elizabeth's mouth as the light above the sliding door went on. Justin concluded the bulb had a light censor that turned it on automatically. But Elizabeth looked in the direction of the door and covered her mouth with her hand. Justin threw a glance at the door, ajar now. He could see half of Serena's face behind the drapes. He turned his attention back to Elizabeth.

"C'mon. Let's move away from the door," he suggested, pressing her elbow.

When they were out of Serena's hearing range, he said, "I know Ramona was raped and not by Willie Oz. She was raped by Ron Patterson, who back in '69 went by the name of Pretty Boy. Patterson and Oz were undercover feds who infiltrated the Third World Liberation Front at Cal, the Black Panther Party and the Crusade for Justice in Denver, among other militant groups. They had carte blanche when it came to their covert activities. But whereas Oz was for the most part a sincere, if mistaken, apostle of J. Edgar Hoover's, Patterson believed in nothing but himself. He felt he could get away with anything, including rape. And he did. Some piece of *mierda!*"

Elizabeth was trying very hard to stop her hands from shaking so much.

Justin took both her cold hands in his and began to rub them gently. "Whose idea was it to break into Oz's house, Gastón's or yours?" he asked.

"I . . . I have no idea what you're talking about. Was there a break-in at Oz's? When?"

Justin looked in her eyes. She was obviously disturbed by his questions, but, as far as he could tell, she was telling the truth. "Oz said that someone broke into his house a couple of months ago and stole some documents, incriminating stuff. If you didn't, then who? Gastón? Could Ramona herself have done it?"

"I haven't the slightest. Ramona has been acting strangely—I mean—weirder than usual. She told me she was writing about what happened to us during the Third World Student Strike, about Irene's birth. For years, she never wanted to talk about what happened back in '69 or the birth of Irene. I tried to get her to talk about all that many times, but she always acted as if she really didn't know what I was talking about. Then suddenly she's asking me all sorts of questions about that time. She was on to something, she told me."

Justin pulled out a patio chair, turned it around, and sat astride it. "She doesn't remember what happened to her? It's been thirty years, but rape is hardly an experience a woman forgets that easily, let alone giving birth to a child."

"I think she went into total denial after it happened. She's been drinking, heavily at times, for at least twenty-five of those years."

"That might be, but as I said, rape is not a walk in a rose garden. . . . No point in going there now. But tell me what happened in '69. Did you know back then that Ramona had been raped, or that she suspected Willie Oz had done it?"

"No. I was never sure of anything." Elizabeth was quiet.

Justin waited out her silence.

"Ramona got very depressed after that confrontation with the cops at U.C., back in February of 1969. I think I told you, she and I both landed at Highland. I was upset, obviously. Who wouldn't be? But Ramona took it harder. She'd start crying for no reason at all. She was so sensitive about everything, anything anyone would say. She's always been petite, but she seemed to be shrinking—withering is a better way to put it. She wasn't eating well, was sleeping little. One day I noticed that her belly was getting bigger while the rest of her was skin and bones. I became suspicious and I asked her point-blank if she was pregnant. She broke down and, after crying her eyes out, she confessed that she was. She had made the mistake of telling her mother that she was. Her mother is a . . . How can I put it?"

"A cold and insensitive woman," Justin said, supplying kinder words than Elizabeth had in mind to describe Lena Serna. "I stopped by the hospital on my way here. I met Mrs. Serna."

"Then you can see why Ramona was so desperate, felt so abandoned. I was her only friend, her only hope. She wanted to have an abortion, she told me. She and I put together our savings, but we couldn't find anyone to do it. In 1969, a woman with an unwanted pregnancy was stuck, or ended up butchered. Too much time went by, so the pregnancy was too advanced for an abortion. I talked to some people in the community who told me about a home for unwed mothers near a hippy farm outside Eureka. Nora Westin, the midwife who ran the place, could arrange for someone to adopt the baby. But Ramona was scared to go there alone. So I took the quarter off at Cal and went with her to Eureka. I got a job at the local McDonald's and rented a room at a boardinghouse near Nora's home.

"The day before Irene was born, Ramona began to have contractions, but they were weak. Before Nora could do anything about it, Ramona ran away from the home. We searched for her all afternoon and evening. To no avail. Then about midnight, she called my boardinghouse. She had checked into a motel. Nora and I went to get her. She was a mess. She'd been drinking and crying for a long time. She kept grabbing my arm, asking me to take the baby when it came. Nora and I were exhausted and took turns watching over her. About six the next morning, Irene was born. Ramona rejected the baby from the start. The baby wouldn't take the bottle. I don't know why, maybe Nora was exhausted or maybe afraid that the baby would die, but she yielded to Ramona's threats that, unless I took the baby as my own, she would let her die. I began to care for Irene, but no one had to force me. I fell in love with Irene the moment I held her in my arms. It didn't take much convincing for me to agree to register her as my own. Nora was a good woman, and she took pity on the baby and Ramona. Risking losing everything she'd worked for, Nora filled out the paperwork and sent it to Eureka. Afterwards, Ramona disappeared for weeks.

"I came back to Oakland with a newborn. I thought my parents were going to be very upset, but they were delighted instead. When they asked, I told them that I'd been afraid to confess I was pregnant and that's why I'd gone away. Later, when I showed them the birth certificate, they accepted my version of the truth. And like me, they also fell in love with Irene. I've thanked God for that unearned blessing every day of Irene's life and mine. I thought, however, that one day Ramona would change her mind and want her daughter back, but she never even mentioned the whole episode. It was almost as if nothing of the sort had ever happened to her.

"Then Ramona began to flirt with suicide. She had never done drugs at Cal. After Irene's birth, she began to experiment with LSD, mescaline, all sorts of other stuff. To increase her creativity, she told me. She was always high on something or other. I don't think she snorts coke or shoots up, but . . . . Anyway, for a long time, Ramona hardly called or talked to me. Then one night, she showed up at my door. I was putting Irene to bed. Ramona was drunk and began to hug Irene, who was barely five years old, and she frightened her. Ramona told her she was sorry for abandoning her. She was suffocating Irene and I had to struggle with her to let Irene go. I put Irene to bed, and Ramona and I got into it. She was screaming at the top of her lungs, so I had to slap her and shove her out the door. In the days after, I kept calling her, but she hung up on me every time. I didn't see her or hear from her for months. One day, she was back at my front door, high on something, and apologizing for not returning my call the day before. I hadn't called her, but I kept quiet. She behaved as if she had no recollection of what had transpired the last time we'd seen each other. She was a mess. But she was my best friend and Irene's mother. I promised myself that, whatever happened, I would not abandon her."

"You still haven't answered my question. Did you suspect that Willie Oz was Irene's father or did Ramona tell you?"

"While Ramona was in labor, almost delirious, she said something about Oz, about the odor of his skin, how she'd wanted him so much and how he'd done this 'terrible thing' to her. I can only guess that she wanted him to make love to her, but that she changed her mind; still, he forced himself on her. Much later, when I asked her about him, Ramona refused to talk about him or anyone else. I never knew for sure who raped her, who was—is—Irene's biological father. Oh, God!"

Elizabeth threw her head back and closed her eyes as she wound up her tale. "What have I done to deserve this grief? When I met Gastón I wanted to be honest with him. I was in love with him. We were about to be married. I told him everything about me, about Ramona and Irene. But he's the one who's lied to me. How could he?"

Justin was quiet for a while. Words were a useless palliative. She had not broken down so far, although he could see the tears welling

up in her eyes. He had stuck a knife in her heart and now was about
to twist it. He hoped she was strong enough to survive the rest. Still,
he weighed the consequences of telling her about Serena or about having found Oz's safe.

Gastón Saucedo would surely demand that Justin turn Oz's documents and journal over to him. What would Gastón do with them?
Protect his family? Use them to blackmail Patterson, to obtain political favors from the would-be assemblyman? Pretty Boy was certainly
in the position to grant them. But, if Oz was right, Patterson was a
ruthless, heartless son-of-a-bitch. He would not just acquiesce to the
blackmail and be done with it. He would come after Saucedo, guns
pointing, and Elizabeth and her daughters would be caught in the
crossfire. Justin was glad that Elizabeth had not inquired further about
the break-in at Oz's house. It was better to let the safe and its contents
remain in Dora's possession for the time being.

"What do you want me to do? Do you want me to find Patterson?
It shouldn't be too hard," Justin asked. He expected Elizabeth to tell
him to proceed with the search.

"I don't know. Hold off until I've had a chance to think about all
this, maybe talk with Gastón," she said.

"What's going to happen to the baby, to Gabi? Why hasn't
Ramona been tested?"

"Ironic, isn't it? I was going to ask her, no, demand that she do it,
have the test and donate the tissue. The least she could do for Gabi and
for Irene. Then, she herself volunteered to get the test done. She had
it done independently—not at Kaiser Hospital, like the rest of us. No
matter, she showed me the results. She isn't a compatible donor. I just
don't know enough about genetics to explain it. So I hired you to find
Oz, thinking that he or one of his children could be compatible. Now
we know that would have been useless, too." Elizabeth stroked her
forehead with her fingers and exhaled.

Justin looked in the direction of the house. Serena was still there,
observing them from behind the curtained window. He turned his
attention to Elizabeth, who was saying, "Why didn't Ramona tell me
all this? She knew Willie wasn't Irene's father. Why didn't she tell me,
do something about finding Patterson? But she never said a word to

me, except to insist she deliver the envelope to Vista Point. She was adamant, and I finally caved in."

"So you never told her you were looking for Willie Oz."

"No. I told her it was a delicate matter that could spoil my chances for a seat in the Oakland City Council. She seemed to be comfortable with my explanation. Now, we don't know if she'll ever snap out of the coma. And Gabi is still at risk. Her immune system gets weaker by the minute. We can't wait much longer. Any opportunistic infection, even a simple cold, could send her into respiratory trauma. If that happens, her chances for survival are next to none."

Elizabeth looked in the direction of the family room. Serena was now standing at the sliding door. Elizabeth raised her hand. With her index finger an inch above her thumb, she signaled for her daughter to wait a while longer.

"Have you ever told Irene about Ramona?"

"No. But when Gabi's problems started, she asked why being the baby's grandmother I could not donate the bone marrow. I tried to explain the medical facts about marrow compatibility. Irene accused me of wanting the baby dead. Then, she told me that when she was little, she overheard my shouting match with Ramona that night I told you about. Irene was so young at the time this happened that I doubt she knew exactly what it all meant. But it must have impacted her tremendously."

"What did you say to Irene when she asked you about her birth?"

"I told her it was true I had adopted her when she was only a few days old, that her birth mother hadn't had the means to support her. Irene was so disturbed by what I told her that she took off with Gabi for a few days. She didn't tell anyone where she was, not even Raymond, her husband. To this day, she still refuses to tell us where she went. We searched for her frantically, but she came back home on her own and never mentioned the facts of her birth again. She's completely devoted to Gabi and Raymond. She was cold towards me, but I knew that once the baby was all right, we would patch up our differences."

"A birth certificate usually says where someone was born. Hers, I'm sure, is no exception. Have you ever considered that she might have gone to Eureka, looking for her birth mother? Did you ask her?"

"I suspect she did just that, but I didn't pursue it. Irene was so emotionally fragile. I was happy she and Gabi were back home. That's all that mattered."

Justin sighed.

Elizabeth looked at him curiously. "There's something else, isn't there? Something you're not telling me. What is it?"

He looked directly at her and said, "A young woman, dressed in black sweats and a ski cap, was seen jogging around Vista Point at the time of Ramona's accident." He looked intently at her.

Elizabeth fixed her eyes on him, too. She frowned and threw her head slightly back. "Oh, God! No! You think that Irene might be that woman. *No.* You're wrong. Rest assured. The baby was running a temperature that day. It was low, but Irene didn't want to take any chances. She took Gabi to Kaiser Hospital. Besides, Irene never wears black. She doesn't even own a pair of socks that color."

There was no point in trying to sweeten bitterness. Bluntly, Justin asked, "Where was Serena the day of Ramona's accident?"

Elizabeth closed her eyes tight. She opened them again and glared at him. "I'm going to forget you asked me that," she said through her clenched teeth.

"I wish you wouldn't. Something is going on with Serena. The time to do right for her is now, before something worse happens. You know me well enough. You must know I wouldn't bring it up if I didn't have any proof."

"What evidence?"

"Someone saw a young woman who looked like Serena in the vicinity of Vista Point at exactly the time of Ramona's accident. She had a . . ."

"Someone who looked like Serena? Really, Justin. Do you really expect me to buy into that, to believe that my seventeen-year-old daughter might have knowingly pushed Ramona over the edge? What would her motive be? Maybe if you tell me why or how, you might convince me."

"I can only tell you that this young woman was dressed in black, she had a key ring . . ."

"Stop right there. Not good enough," Elizabeth interjected, waving her hand in the air. "This is preposterous." She ran her fingers through her hair. Looking at him directly, she commanded, "Drop the investigation. I'll go to Patterson myself. Get on my knees and beg him. Drop it." Elizabeth turned to walk back into the house.

Justin grabbed hold of her arm and made her face him. "*Estás loca*. No way in hell you're going to Patterson. Promise me. I don't think you really realize the kind of man he is. Do you really think you're going to convince him and he'll just admit it and donate the bone marrow? He's a criminal. Get that through your head. Stay away from him. And what about Serena and Irene?"

She squinted and freed herself from his grip. She seemed calm, too calm.

"I told you before, but let me assure you again. Neither Serena nor Irene are capable of doing anything like you're suggesting. Drop the investigation. Okay?"

Elizabeth began to walk back into the house. This time, Justin did not stop her. He followed her in.

Serena, who had been watching them all along, walked quickly to the sofa and lay on it. She began to flip through the TV channels.

As they stepped in, the phone rang, and Elizabeth walked to the kitchen to take the call.

"Hmmm. I wonder what Gastón's going to say when I tell him about you and my mother," Serena said. "Secrets, oh so many secrets. Life with Mother," she added, looking Justin over.

It was the kind of look that compels a woman to check her attire and a man to discreetly make sure his pants are zipped up. When Justin did not react the way she expected, she arched her brows and glared at him.

Justin considered leaving things alone, as Elizabeth had told him, but he knew he could not do that, not as long as Ramona was still in a coma, not as long as Oz was looking for his safe, and Vincent Constantino was still missing. Things had already been set in motion and they would play themselves out, whether he made them his business or not. The only way to avert tragedy was to deal with Serena and Gastón, find a way to deter Elizabeth from contacting Patterson directly, then stop Oz before he had a chance to deal with Patterson.

Dora, he was sure, would find Vincent Constantino.

Taking advantage of being alone with Serena, he said, "You like Barbie dolls and black jogging outfits." He waited a couple of seconds, then tagged the comment, "Don't you?"

She waved him off, pressed a button on the remote control to change channels again, and turned the volume up.

Raising his voice over the loud music, he said, "Be careful when you jog. A friend of mine, a private investigator, had a bad experience with a man who attacked her recently. He was carrying a pepper spray container. Now she carries one, just like yours. Good idea. You never know when you're going to need it."

Serena sat up, then lay back down on the sofa. "Whatever. I don't give a fuck about your friend. Or about you."

"You should be careful, though. There's a man, a Mexican cowboy, who likes you. He'll never forget your face, he told me."

Serena avoided looking at him, but Justin could see her eyes moving rapidly side to side.

"Beware. You just might have bitten off more than you can chew," Justin warned as Elizabeth walked back into the family room.

"Fax me your invoice. I'll send you a check by return mail."

"Thanks." He lowered his voice on purpose. "By the way, do you know a Vincent Constantino?"

As he expected, Serena began to lower the volume.

"No. Who is he?"

"He's a writer. He claims he's located Oz's safe. He'll be meeting me at my office at eight this evening."

"Please, Justin. Leave it alone." Elizabeth walked to the front door and held the door open for Justin.

Justin threw a glance in Serena's direction. The young woman sat cross-legged on the sofa, seemingly enthralled by Ricky Martin's 'Vida Loca' MTV routine. But Justin could tell she was looking at him out of the corner of her eye.

Elizabeth refused to even look at him. He heard the door slam shut behind him. He got in his car, turned his cell phone on, and checked for messages. Dora had called. She would have to wait. He looped around the driveway. He waved at Gastón's security man, who was leaning on an old Continental. He turned right onto the street and looked for Oz's van where he had last seen him. Oz had probably left after Gastón's security man had gotten to the house. One thing less to worry about now.

Justin drove slowly down the street. He prayed that Serena would not follow, that Elizabeth would be spared the grief. But the headlights of the metallic blue Mustang behind him confirmed to him that his prayer had not been answered.

SEVENTEEN
A Taste for Fear

A SPECTACULAR OCHER-COLORED moon was beginning to rise over the Oakland hills when Dora noticed for the first time the brown Dodge van shadowing her every move.

She was driving down Park Boulevard on her way home. Two hours earlier, Justin had phoned her from his office, saying he was going to Highland Hospital, then to Elizabeth's house. He was sure Oz, who as usual was parked outside his office, would follow. So Dora felt safe dropping off a copy of Oz's materials at Justin's office. As Justin had requested, she called him from his office, but he was not answering his phone. She left a message for him, saying she would be heading home as soon as she did some grocery shopping at the Safeway down the street. She picked up two books on the Crusade for Justice that Justin had left for her to read. She looked at the books, *The Crusade for Justice* by Ernesto Vigil and *The Ultimate Betrayal* by Juan Haro. She put the books in her handbag and left the office.

Now, Oz was after her. This fed was as good as they come. Or she and Justin were not covering all the bases.

Dora kept an eye on the brown Dodge van. At the corner with Monterey Avenue she turned right. Oz followed. She reached for her phone and punched Justin's cell phone number again. This time, he picked up the call.

"Whatever you do, don't mention my name or what this is about," Dora warned when Justin answered.

Justin acquiesced to her request with an "Uh-huh."

"Guess what? I picked up a tail. This Oz guy doesn't know me from Eve, so why is he now following me? Question one. Two. Could he have followed you to my place earlier this afternoon?"

"Not possible. I personally checked and double-checked the invoice."

"That leaves only one possibility. Your place is bugged. I know you checked your van already. If I were you, I'd check everywhere at home and office, just in case."

Justin shook his head. Damn! He had thought about that possibility before, but he had done nothing about it. He was getting too careless. To Dora, he said, "Yes, I see. I must have overlooked those two items. Thanks." Justin looked around his office, already trying to figure out where Oz could have planted electronic listening devices.

"I'll lose this guy," Dora said. "I'll be at home if you need to reach me."

"It's okay to bring the item in question, with copies of the invoices," Justin said. "My office at eight this evening?"

"Bring the safe? Are you sure?"

"Right. I'll have the invoice ready by then."

She had no idea what Justin was planning to do. Right now she needed a plan to get Oz off her tail. She drove slowly down Monterey Avenue, then turned right again on Thirty-fifth Avenue. She followed Thirty-fifth until she saw the entrance to the MacArthur Freeway. She took the ramp onto the freeway heading west.

Although the traffic was not particularly heavy on the MacArthur, she knew the traffic would increase when they approached the Maze, the area where the MacArthur split in two, west to San Francisco and east towards Berkeley and Sacramento. After the 1989 Loma Prieta earthquake, with the collapse of many sections of freeways, the Maze had become the juncture of all freeways in the East Bay. Traffic on it had multiplied. She did not want to get trapped in that area, with Oz right on her heels. Dora saw the sign for the downtown loop, one of the last two exits before the Maze. She had a mile and a half to make her move.

The downtown exit ramp was already in sight. Dora's heart began to race. Her ears buzzed and her belly tightened as blood pressure rose in anticipation of the chase, each one of her senses keenly aware of danger and survival. Her mouth tasted as if she had rubbed her tongue with copper—fear mixed with excitement, the taste of the thrill. She was becoming addicted to that powerful combination. But that did not mean she had to be reckless, she reminded herself.

She checked the traffic in the lane to the right of her, watching for an opportune moment. The close call was going to be the delivery truck inching its way on the far right lane towards the downtown Oakland exit.

Without checking on Oz's van, Dora stepped on the gas and weaved through traffic as fast as possible until she reached the lane next to the exit. She would have to cut right in front of the delivery truck, with less than a few feet between it and her car.

The taste of fear rushed with her spit down her throat as she paralleled the truck. She took a few quick breaths, pressed the gas pedal, clenched her teeth, and veered into exit position. She took the exit ramp with only a foot between her car and the guardrail. She stepped on the gas once again, then pumped her brake to slow down and not hit the car ahead of hers. Air gushed out of her mouth.

She checked her mirrors. There was not even a hint of brown behind her. She took a deep breath and relaxed her grip on the steering wheel. She even smiled at the righteously indignant delivery driver when he gave her the finger.

She got off the downtown loop on Twelfth Street, circled around and entered the MacArthur heading east—home. Every so often, she checked to make sure Oz was not following her. Thank God, she and Justin had not mentioned her name or address when they had previously talked. Oz had no way of tracking her down in such a short time.

Forty-five minutes later, she was home. Her heart was still dancing a furious Mexican *zapateado* in her chest. The taste of adrenaline still flooded every taste bud and nasal membrane. She drank some water to flush the taste of fear down, then fixed herself a pot of coffee. She gulped down the first cup and took a refill to her office. In an hour, she would have to meet with Justin. She had no idea what his plan was, but she was sure it was hardly going to be a slumber party.

She sipped her coffee as she poured over Oz's field journal, trying to confirm an idea beginning to germinate in her mind. She skipped all the entries that talked about Oz's activities in the Bay Area and concentrated instead on his and Pretty Boy's activities in Denver. The pair had been very busy there, as had other law enforcement agencies, ranging from the local Denver police Department to the FBI, ATF, and even the CIA.

About the Crusade for Justice, Oz had written: "A movement like the Crusade for Justice, headed by Rodolfo 'Corky' Gonzales, an ex-boxer, ex-Democratic politician, strong charismatic Mexican-American community organizer, has become the central concern of every law enforcement agency in the United States. The Crusade has also attracted a great number of young people from all over the United States who believe that the time has come for Mexican Americans to look America in the eye and spit in her face. They rise in protest. They aim to arm themselves if necessary. They want their voices heard, their presence noted, even if by violent means.

"It isn't that I find their demands unfair. Racism exists. No doubt about it. But those demands will soon be forgotten. Eventually, all of these organizations will be victims of their own hunger for power. Power fucks up everything and J. Edgar's soldiers will be there to make sure it does. No difference between an LSD trip and a power trip. Both lead you to believe you can fly. They let you believe you cannot die. Therein the downfall of Corky Gonzales, or El Caudillo, as he's called by his lieutenants. Gonzales makes J. Edgar's chubby fingers itch and his perfectly coifed hair stand on end. Hoover is afraid there will be one leader—and it takes only one—who will unite all these subversive groups under one banner, one cause. I'm sure it ain't going to happen. Students of history, these people ain't. Determined, yes, even if fools, all of them. No way they can win an armed struggle. But like the ants on the burning log, they will follow the leader down to hell itself. They just don't know yet there is no way out of it."

Reading Oz's personal observations, Dora wondered how it all had been back in the sixties. When the Chicano civil rights movement picked up momentum back then, she was only a toddler in Texas. Like many of her Mexican-American college classmates, she admired the accomplishments of that first generation of Chicanos who had dared to challenge a racist caste system. She was grateful, for without them, she and many other Chicanos would not be looking forward to a brighter future. Despite her feelings of gratitude and her admiration, she regarded Chicano militancy and nationalistic ideology as a thing of the past—history. It must have been exciting, though, to have that kind of hope, to fight for it, she mused as she read the newspaper clippings Oz had collected.

The clippings—from Chicano newspapers, Dora realized—reported on activities during the Crusade-sponsored Youth Conferences and "Fishermen's meetings." Fishermen's meetings! Really! It sounded to Dora like Corky Gonzales saw himself as Christ the Savior. Many of the women from the California contingent did not think he was. The Chicano movement was male-oriented, and Oz had underlined the names of women who had questioned the traditional role the Crusade continued to impose on them. None of the names of Patterson's rape victims were among them.

Another clipping offered a rave review of the wedding of one of Corky Gonzales's daughters during one of the conferences. One of the best-attended weddings ever. The details of the wedding made it sound as if royalty had gotten married. It seemed to Dora as if the Gonzaleses of Denver had been regarded as a Chicano royal family. People seemed to worship them. Corky Gonzales was handsome, strong, brave, admired in the community, respected and protected by his loyal "fishermen." His wife was committed to the cause; his children were young adults, good-looking, urban, and smart.

Dora skimmed the rest of the clippings. She decided to skip them and went back to Oz's journal.

In Denver, Pretty Boy had gone wild. He had become more and more daring. He hung out openly with some of the meanest local cops and feds. He and another local cop had running bets as to how many *señoritas* each was going to lay. Willie Oz's contempt for Pretty Boy was obvious in his writings. It was also evident that he had begun to distance himself from Pretty Boy.

Dora looked closely at the photos of the three Denver young women who had been raped by Pretty Boy. She pulled out a magnifying glass from her desk drawer and studied the pictures carefully. She then pulled out the photos of Jesse Latour. What if he was the ill-conceived child of one of Pretty Boy's rape victims? But which of these three women? Had he also been put up for adoption? If he had been adopted in the United States, he would have remained in the country. From what Luis Móntez had told her, Latour had indicated that he had been born in the United States but had lived abroad. Felicia, the Chilean foreign student at Boulder—she could be Latour's mother. Dora wished Oz had also written their last names.

How and why had Vincent Constantino become acquainted with Latour's case? Who had told him about it? Her intuition told her she was on the right track. But every road led back to Vincent Constantino, and, by default, to Ramona M. Serna, neither of whom was available to unravel the mystery.

It was getting closer to eight. Dora pulled off the FBI file jackets and put her own copy of Oz's files in them. She locked away the journal and original FBI files in a desk drawer. She got a waist holster and fastened it to her belt, then put the gun in it and secured it. She reached into her handbag for her wallet and put it in her jacket pocket. She wheeled the box containing her own copies of the materials and the empty safe out and locked the front door. She loaded box and safe into her car trunk, then returned the materials to the safe and locked it.

When Dora was ready to take off, she saw Beatrice stepping out the front door of the main house. Dora stopped and lowered the passenger window. "I'll call you tomorrow," she shouted and waved.

Beatrice made the sign of the cross in the air.

EIGHTEEN
Fed Bugs

JUSTIN ARRIVED HOME. Serena had taken the bait and followed him. As he crossed his driveway towards his flat, he threw a quick glance around. He was not sure where Serena had parked or if she had at all. Perhaps she intended to come back later on. He hoped not. The young woman was resourceful and bold, he had to grant her that. But she had no idea what and who she was up against. Oz's van was not anywhere in sight. He had not heard from Dora, but he hoped she had been able to shake Oz off her tail. It was six-thirty in the evening. She would be arriving at eight as agreed, with the safe in plain sight.

After drawing the curtains in the front room, he turned on the lights. A meticulous search of his living quarters yielded no electronic listening devices. He reached into the fridge for a Coke and retrieved his flashlight from a kitchen drawer, then walked up the stairs to his office.

The blinds in his office were closed, as he had left them. He remembered seeing some objects out of place there. A torchiere lamp and a two-shelf bookcase were slightly off their indented mark on the carpet and a file drawer had been left ajar. He checked them first. Twenty minutes later he had easily detected three bugs in his office. Oz must have planted them sometime in the dead of night, when Justin was having a death dream. Justin had thought that Gloria had been the person making noises upstairs, perhaps taking care of last minute details before her trip to Lake Tahoe. Now he knew better.

For someone with such finesse as unlocking a door without a scratch to the wood or metal, Oz had been negligent in tidying up after himself.

Justin opened the blinds. He pulled a chair to the window and sat there in the dark, sipping his Coke, keeping an eye on the action or lack of it outside. At fifteen minutes before eight, he called Dora's house. There was no answer. He left a message for her, in which he clearly mentioned the safe and their meeting at his office at eight. If Oz was somewhere nearby, listening, he would show up at the appointed hour.

Ten minutes later, he watched Oz's van drive down Fruitvale Avenue. From his place at the window, Justin could not see where the old fed parked but he was sure it was not too far away. Justin had to admit that he was intrigued by the guy. Oz was definitely a walking contradiction: an obsolete, old and dying operative, forever rolling up and down the arc of an ethical question mark. Perhaps that was why Justin's office had more bugs than a basement pantry, but his flat was clean.

Reading Oz's account of his undercover activities during the sixties and seventies, Justin realized that agents like Oz knew things about individuals and organizations no one else had been privy to. Oz knew where all the political bodies on both sides were buried. But, no matter how intrigued Justin was by Oz, the old fed was his adversary, and Justin would bring him down if he had to.

Justin scanned the traffic on Fruitvale Avenue. He saw Serena's metallic blue Mustang pulling into a parking spot twenty-five feet from his house. He noticed an old Lincoln Continental pull into another spot across the street. The driver did not get out. "Gastón's man," Justin said under his breath. Except for Dora, all the players were in place.

Justin expected Dora to show up with the safe at any minute. What he did not expect was to see Elizabeth's BMW pull into his driveway a few minutes later. She parked right behind his van and popped open the trunk of her car. She quickly walked to the rear of her car and retrieved a box from the trunk. Then, she started running towards Justin's flat.

Justin skipped down the stairs, leaving the connecting door between the two floors ajar. He was already at the door when Elizabeth rang the bell. She was pale and short of breath. The redness saw Dora standing there with the safe strapped to a hand truck. He rushed to help her and closed the door again. He wheeled the safe next to the table.

He made the introductions. Dora shook Elizabeth's hand, then joined Justin at the table. "What's going on? Why is she here?" she whispered.

"Unexpected developments. Her youngest daughter Serena was the woman seen at Vista Point." He pointed at the box of clothes next to the safe. Dora began to inspect the clothes.

He had just turned to join Elizabeth in the living room when the doorbell rang. "Company," he told Dora without turning. He tugged a bewildered but reluctant Elizabeth to the door leading up to his office. He pushed on her until she was completely out of sight. "Run upstairs, wait a short while, then get out as quickly as you can." He pushed the door closed and put his ear to the door. He did not hear Elizabeth's footsteps, but there was no time to check on her. He leaped over to the front door.

Dora took her gun out and got behind the dining table. She aimed her gun at the door and signaled for Justin to open it.

As soon as the door opened, Oz stepped in. He cleared the door and Justin pushed it shut. Oz turned his head slightly to take a look at him.

"Hands up where I can see them," Dora commanded. She was surprised to see that Oz did not have a gun. "Keep them up."

Justin walked over to Oz and frisked him briefly.

Oz smiled. "I'm not packing," he said. "Tell the Brown Angel here to relax."

Dora could not help but admire his bravado. But, perhaps his was not courage. Fearlessness, most likely, the last trench of valor when death had the upper hand, she thought. But she did not lower her weapon.

"I see you found my safe. I knew you would. I'm sure you know what's in it now. You, too, Brown Angel?" he asked, addressing Dora. "Good driving."

She nodded.

Oz turned to Justin and asked, "What now?"

around her watery eyes spelled fear and anguish. Justin was sure th trouble she carried in that cardboard box was heavy. He took it fro her and ushered her in.

"You were right," Elizabeth said as Justin set the box down on th dining room table. Elizabeth pulled out two long-sleeved extra-larg black sweatshirts and sweat pants, and two ski masks. "You wer telling me things about my daughters. I had to be sure that everythin was as I said with Irene and Serena, so I went to Irene's place."

"And you found all these clothes at Irene's?"

"Yes. I found them in a closet in her house."

"What did Irene say about them?"

Elizabeth put the clothes back in the box. "I didn't talk to her about them. Raymond's mother was taking care of Gabi. Irene need-ed a break, and Raymond took her out to dinner. I found the box and came directly here. You've got to help me. What's going on? Please tell me everything, don't spare me any details, no matter how painful."

"All right. You were right about Irene. I think she might know something about Ramona's so-called accident, but she was not the woman seen near Vista Point. Serena was. I'm sure of it. Take my word for it."

"Whew! This is too much." Elizabeth stretched her arm back until she touched the back of the sofa. She lowered herself slowly to the sofa, like someone whose every muscle ached. She rubbed her tem-ples. "I just can't believe it. Serena?"

Justin sat down next to her. He took her hands in his. "This is important. Think hard. How could Serena know about Ramona's ren-dezvous with the messenger at Vista Point, if you didn't tell her? Did Gastón tell her?"

How could Justin do this to her? She gave him a furious look and yanked her hands out of his. "Are you making this up as you go along? What are you saying now? That Gastón is behind all this? That he used my—our daughter——to push Ramona over the edge? You're wrong. He wouldn't. You're making him sound like a conniving, heartless man. He isn't. It makes no sense. No sense."

Justin heard noises outside the front door. He pulled out his gun. Then he heard the key turn in the lock. The door was pushed open. He

"Now, you answer my questions."

"Shoot," Oz said and chuckled. "But make it fast. As you know, I'm running out of time."

"Did Pretty Boy rape Ramona Serna?"

Oz looked down and nodded.

"Why is it that you didn't say anything about it in your field log?"

"I had no idea he intended to rape Ramona. Believe me." Oz closed his eyes. "I felt bad." He opened his eyes and looked directly at Justin. He shook his head. "She'd been hit by a sheriff's deputy. She seemed disoriented. When Patterson suggested we get her out of there, I agreed. I liked Ramona. I'd read her poems. Of all that bunch, she was the only one worth saving. I thought Patterson had taken pity on her, too. I found out too late he hadn't. I tried to fight him off, but he drew his weapon on me, got in the car with her, and locked the doors." He sighed. "I got out of there. Only time I wondered what the hell I was doing, getting myself involved in all that. I couldn't write about it without implicating myself. The rule of the jungle: *Me* first. *Mine* second."

"So much for courage under fire," Dora said.

"Right about that, Angel."

"You mentioned three women in Denver who were raped by Patterson. Do you know if any of those women got pregnant or had a baby after the rape?" Dora asked.

Oz thought for a moment, then shook his head. He glanced at Justin, then at Dora. "No more questions?"

Oz began to cough. Dora saw him cover his mouth with one hand while he reached down to his ankle with the other.

"Make another move and you're dead! C'mon. Take *it* out. Slowly," she commanded. The man had to be crazy attempting anything with two guns pointed at him.

"Easy, Angel," Oz said, but he did not remove his hand from his ankle.

"C'mon, man. Do you really want to do that? What about your kids? Don't they deserve the *insurance* money?" Justin reasoned.

Oz raised the leg of his pants slowly and unstrapped a .22 from his ankle. He put it on the floor. Justin stepped forward and pushed the gun out of the way with his shoe.

Oz got up slowly. He began to walk towards the safe, still strapped to the dolly. Dora stepped back and circled around the table, her gun aimed at him all the time. "At ease, Divine Creature," he said. He pushed the dolly around and began to wheel it out with Dora following him at a safe distance away.

Justin backed up towards the connecting door. He opened it. Elizabeth was no longer behind it. He took the steps up by two. She was not in his office either. The outside door to his office was open. He checked the driveway. Elizabeth's car was still there. He shut the door and made sure it was locked, then skipped down the outside staircase and looked in the BMW. He saw Dora standing on the sidewalk, keeping an eye on Oz as the old fed attempted and failed to load the safe into his van. He rushed to the spot.

"Cover me," Dora said as she slid her gun between her pants waist and back. "The sooner he leaves, the better off we'll all be." She helped Oz.

Justin kept an eye on Dora and Oz, sneaking a look out for Elizabeth. He finally spotted her, talking with Serena. She must have seen her daughter's Mustang and gone to find out what Serena was doing there. The man in the Lincoln was there, too. When Dora was out of harm's way, Justin rushed up to the mother and daughter.

Elizabeth was saying, "You have a lot of explaining to do. You'd better start *now!*" Her nostrils were flared, her voice scaled up.

Serena smirked, raised her eyebrows, and cupped her hands over her ears.

Elizabeth took her by the shoulders and began to shake her. Saucedo's security man approached and reached out. Elizabeth pushed his hand away. "And you, Tom, what are you doing here? Did Gastón send you? How did you know where to find her?" Her fist was close to Tom's chin.

Tom backed off and raised his arms. "Mr. Saucedo called me and told me where Serena was. I'm just doing my job, Mrs. Saucedo."

Justin looked Tom over. He was in shirtsleeves and his pants pockets were not bulging. "Let them talk it out," Justin suggested.

Tom acquiesced with a nod of his head.

"How did my husband know where she was?"

Tom shrugged his shoulders.

"Did you call Gastón? Why?" Elizabeth asked Serena.

Serena seemed unfazed by her mother's anger. But her scornful eyes spoke for her.

"It's about Irene, isn't it? Isn't it?" Elizabeth's voice rose. "You've always been jealous of her. That's it. You're out to get her. For God's sake! She's your sister!"

"Jealous of her? Wake up, Mommy. Whose idea do you think it was? All this time your wonderful Irene plots against you. You make my stomach turn."

Furious, Elizabeth slapped Serena. Serena cried out. Tom grabbed Serena's arm before she had a chance to strike back.

"Bitch!" Serena said as she pushed Tom out of the way. Tom stumbled against Justin. They both fell down.

Serena got in her car and started the engine. Elizabeth stepped in front of her daughter's car and put both her hands on the hood. Serena revved the engine. Elizabeth stood her ground.

Justin and Tom scrambled to their feet. Justin grabbed Elizabeth by her waist and began to pull her away towards the sidewalk. Tom ran to his car and got in.

Serena backed her car up and sped out of the parking spot with a screech. Tom took off after her. Elizabeth fell on her knees and began to sob.

Justin and Dora helped her up and across the street. They were walking back into Justin's flat when Elizabeth's cell phone rang.

Elizabeth took the call. "I'll be home soon," she said flatly and turned the receiver off. She now seemed to be extremely calm, but Dora was sure the storm was still raging inside her.

"Oz is going to be one pissed fed when he discovers he's been given a pussycat, not a tiger. We better get out of here quickly," Dora told Justin, looking at her watch.

"Can you drive home?" he asked Elizabeth.

She looked at him directly and nodded.

"I'll drive ahead. You cover the rear," Justin told Dora. "When we get there, park outside. Keep an eye out for Oz."

As Dora waited for Elizabeth and Justin to back out of the driveway, she heard the whistle of a train, inching its way towards Oakland. She sighed. What she would give to be on that train now.

NINETEEN
In the Whirl of Evidence

THE CONVOY ARRIVED at the Saucedos' house. Justin and Elizabeth drove up the driveway. Dora went past the house and turned around. She found the darkest place, with a clear view of both sides of the street and the driveway, and parked.

Justin saw Serena's Mustang parked down the driveway, behind a Toyota. Elizabeth drove into her garage. Justin circled around the driveway and parked by the entrance, facing the street. As he walked to the front door, where Elizabeth and Gastón already waited, he spotted Tom's Lincoln Continental parked behind the hedges.

He followed Gastón and Elizabeth to the family room. Serena and Irene, side by side, waited for their parents. Irene shivered and pulled her sweater around her. Serena kept her eyes fixed on Gastón, watching his every move. Gastón had his arms around Elizabeth's shoulders and seemed very solicitous towards his wife. Serena showed nothing but contempt for her mother. More trouble ahead for Elizabeth, Justin thought.

"Where's Gabi?" Elizabeth asked Irene.

"At home, with Raymond," she answered but did not look at her mother. Elizabeth ignored Serena, who glared at her from her seat on the arm of the sofa.

Elizabeth settled into an armchair and looked at her husband, then at her daughters. She seemed in control of herself and the situation. "Okay. I'm here. I'm listening."

Gastón eyed Justin.

"Justin stays," Elizabeth told her husband.

Gastón seemed more surprised than upset, but did not voice a protest. He made no move to sit down, resting his hands, instead, on the back of an armchair for support. He glanced briefly at Irene and Serena. Turning his attention to Elizabeth, he finally asked, "What do you want to know?"

"Oh, no. This isn't going to be an interrogation. We're not going to play the good-guy/bad-guy game. You and my daughters have been keeping secrets from me. Heaven knows what else has been going on behind my back."

"We're not the only ones keeping secrets, Mommy." Serena looked at Gastón and Irene for approval. They ignored her remark altogether. She smirked, then slid down onto the sofa, pouting.

"Well. Here's your chance," Elizabeth told Irene. "Tell me that I've been a bad mother, that I've kept you from your *real* mother."

Irene lowered her eyes and kept them fixed on some indistinct spot on the rug.

"I couldn't have loved you more if I'd carried you in my womb for nine months. I was there when you cried, when you were sick or hungry, before, during, and after Gabi was born. I gave you a father when you needed one. Two fathers. Maybe I made the wrong choices . . ." Elizabeth said. Her voice broke. She swallowed hard, trying to contain the tears, but it was difficult to keep them from flowing freely. Gastón offered her his handkerchief. She took it and patted her eyes and cheeks dry.

"Sob, sob, sob," Serena cracked.

"I love you, too, very much, though you've chosen for some confounding reason not to believe it," Elizabeth told Serena. She fixed her teary eyes on Gastón. "You've broken my heart." To her daughters: "All of you."

Irene joined her sister on the sofa. She looked around, like a wounded doe waiting for the fatal shot. Serena looked at Gastón. He signaled for her to be quiet.

Taking advantage of the pause, Justin moved away from the frozen group in the family room to call Dora. She informed him that Oz was there. He had cased the house, but had gotten discouraged after seeing Saucedo's guard outside. Oz seemed to be biding his time.

A few minutes later, Justin rejoined the group. No one seemed to have moved.

Gastón was the first to show signs of life. He walked to Elizabeth and tried to put his arms around her.

Elizabeth, gently but firmly, pushed him away. "Too late for hugs and kisses. I need an explanation."

"It's all my fault," Irene said. "I'm the one who started all this." She gasped for breath.

"It's all right," Gastón told Irene. "Let me tell your mom what happened."

"No, Dad. Mother's right." Irene looked at Elizabeth. "I owe you so much . . . my life. When I went to Eureka, I looked for that Nora Westin; her name was on my birth certificate as the attending midwife. All I had to do was look in the phone book. She was listed. I went to see her. She was very old and had been ill for a long time. I guess by now she's dead. She remembered Ramona and you, Mother. How could she forget you or me, she told me. She'd broken the law to save me. Then she told me about you and Ramona, that Ramona was my birth mother. Before I came home, I went to see Ramona. She was drunk, incoherent. She said something about my father, my biological father, and that she had seen a man recently in Oakland. Some other things I couldn't understand. I begged her to tell me who my father was. She just kept repeating, 'The bastard. The bastard.' But she refused to tell me anything else. I came home, all confused, angry with you. A few days later, it occurred to me Ramona could be the donor we were looking for. After all, she was Gabi's grandmother. I went back to see her and asked her to get tested. She freaked out and began to throw things around. Hadn't you told me? She kept asking, but wouldn't tell me what it was you were supposed to tell me. Then she told me that my father was the perfect donor, she was sure. She told me she'd find him for me. I wanted to believe her. I did. She begged me not to tell anyone, especially you, Mother. What was it you didn't tell me?"

"Ramona was already tested. She herself had the test done. She's not compatible. I tried to tell you it's not that easy to find a compatible donor, not with bone marrow. Not even among blood relatives. That's when we—Gastón and I—decided to find your biological father, and we hired Justin here to do just that. You should have trusted me, regardless of what Ramona told you," Elizabeth said.

"I know I should've, but I was so angry at you. I'm sorry. Ramona called me a few days later. She told me she'd found the man she was looking for. He was living in Oakland. She was going to find my father for me and convince him to get tested. She had something—a safe, she said—to use in case he didn't consent to the test. A man named Vincent, a writer, was keeping the safe for her." Irene rubbed her hair. She began to cry. "It was all so confusing. I begged her to tell me where I could find him. If I could just talk to him, convince him . . . no one had to know about it. She refused. I was at the end of my rope. I couldn't tell Raymond about this, because I was afraid he would confront my biological father and scare him away. I had no one to turn to."

"But you turned to Dad," Elizabeth said and looked at Gastón.

"Not at first. I broke down one day and told Serena. She told Dad. Dad said he would take care of everything. He said he had a very good idea who the man—my biological father—was. I don't know how, but Dad also found out who the writer was that Ramona had talked about."

"How did you find all that out?" Elizabeth said, looking directly at Gastón.

Gastón knelt down beside his wife. "I had Tom follow Ramona. One of those times, he followed her to Vincent Constantino's apartment."

Justin, who had quietly listened to everyone's story, finally spoke. Talking to Gastón, he said, "But neither you nor Tom broke into Vincent's apartment looking for the safe." Turning to Serena and Irene, he asked, "Who did? You or you?"

Irene shook her head but looked askance at her sister.

Serena bolted to her feet. "I did. No one knew what they were doing." She faced Elizabeth. "You convinced Dad to hire a private detective. A good for nothing, if you ask me. I did a better job than he did." Glaring at Justin, she added, "A P.I./Ph! He should take lessons from me." She stood in the middle of the room with her legs apart as if to accept a challenge issued directly at her.

If the situation had not been so serious, Justin would have found her childish posturing amusing.

"What did you do, Serena?" Gastón and Elizabeth asked in unison.

"I took care of business. I heard Dad talk to Tom many times. I went to see Ramona, too. I told her to help Irene or else. Why do you think she agreed to go to Vista Point?"

Elizabeth rose to her feet slowly. "Or else, what?" She leaned on Gastón. "Did you . . . push Ramona over the rail? Please tell me you didn't."

Serena said nothing. She stood there, smiling, her head bobbing.

Everyone's eyes were on Serena, but no one uttered a word. Serena looked at the horror and fear in their eyes and took a few steps back, bumping into the sofa. She moved to the side.

Elizabeth fell to her knees, her mouth and eyes open in disbelief, but it was obvious she was not getting enough air in. Gastón helped her up and made her sit on the sofa. Irene ran to the kitchen to get a glass of water.

Justin looked at Serena. Her livid face and the anguish in her eyes told of a frightened, whimpering little girl.

"I just wanted to make sure she was there. I saw her miss her step. She hit the rail. I ran to help her. I tried to grab her shirt but it was too late. I couldn't save her. I was the one who called nine-one-one later. I did . . . Mommy. Dad."

No one but Justin was paying attention to her. Serena retreated towards the door. Justin approached her cautiously. Serena saw him come closer and turned. Before Justin could grab a hold of her, she ran to the front door, picking up her keys from the table at the entrance on her way out.

Gastón was the first to notice what was going on. He reached into his pocket to call his security men.

"Don't," Justin shouted, heading for the front door. "You'll need them. Oz is coming after you all. He's out there. I'll bring your daughter back home."

By the time he went out the front door, Serena had already taken off, circled the driveway, heading for the street.

He punched Dora's phone number. "Serena's leaving. Don't let her out of your sight. I'll be right behind you."

TWENTY
Fate's Iron Horse

DORA KEPT AN EYE ON OZ'S BROWN VAN, parked on the same side as the Saucedos' home, opposite her. Except for an initial effort to find a point of entry into the residence, Oz sat in his van, waiting, like her.

Her phone rang. Justin was at the other end checking in. Dora told him about Oz. An hour later, her phone rang again. She knew it had to be Justin when she saw Serena, dressed in a blue nightgown and robe, bolt out the front door. She got into her Mustang.

Dora turned the key in the ignition and got her car in gear, but she left the headlights off. She had plenty of room to get out of the parking spot without having to back out. When she saw the Mustang coming down the driveway, she started out slowly. She saw Oz's headlights turn on as soon as he detected the Mustang. Oh, the devil, Dora thought. If Oz caught Serena, he would surely try to trade her for the original contents of his safe. But only over her dead body, Dora told herself.

Serena turned onto the street and moved fast in the opposite direction from Oz's van. He had to maneuver out of the spot and turn about to follow Serena. Dora took advantage of his predicament and stepped on the gas, passing in front of the van seconds before he completed the maneuver.

A cat-and-mouse game followed. Dora managed to keep ahead of him. She checked the rearview mirror, hoping to spot Justin's van. He was too far away to provide any help.

The traffic began to get heavier as they approached the commercial area on Lakeshore Avenue. Dora saw the traffic light turn yellow. Serena was almost at the intersection and sped through it. Dora had to go through the red light. She looked in the rearview mirror. Oz's van had been hit by an AC Transit bus. She hoped the damage to the van was considerable. Her hopes died soon enough as she saw the van take off again. At least they had gained some distance from him.

Serena roller-coasted the sloping hills towards Grand Avenue. The Mustang's brake lights flashed closer to the Grand Avenue intersection. Dora thought Serena was getting ready to stop. Instead, the young woman pushed on and began a sharp left turn against the stoplight. The Mustang sideswiped another car moving through the intersection. The impacted car seemed disabled but not the Mustang.

Traffic on both sides came to a halt. Dora shifted to a lower gear. The engine heaved. But she was able to maneuver through the narrow space between two cars and head down Grand Avenue. She spotted the Mustang turning right onto the ramp to the MacArthur Freeway towards the Maze. She sped up to shorten the distance.

Serena zigzagged through traffic and soon was cruising down the fast lane at eighty-five miles an hour. Dora was thankful that the late evening traffic on the MacArthur was lighter than usual. She stayed in the middle lane, in case Serena decided to go across the Bay Bridge towards San Francisco. She checked her mirrors. Neither Oz's nor Justin's vehicles were anywhere in sight. She eased her grip on the steering wheel to alleviate the cramps in her hands, neck, and shoulders.

Suddenly, Serena began to cut across the freeway toward the downtown Oakland loop exit.

"What is it about this exit?" Dora asked under her breath, recalling her hair-raising race to get away from Oz earlier that day. She eased into the exit lane right behind the Mustang. Serena took the Twelfth Street exit, zigzagging through the deserted streets toward the waterfront, slowing down, then speeding up again as soon as Dora made the turns. Dora surmised the young woman had concluded Dora posed no threat. Serena was now the cat playing with the mouse.

Dora kept an eye out for Oz. Seemingly, he was no longer following them. But she was sure she had not seen the last of him and wondered where the old fed would turn up again.

Serena entered the vacant parking lot of the Cost Plus imports store on Clay Street. She parked in the middle of it, but did not turn off her headlights.

Dora parked at the curb between the entrance and exit to the store lot, across from the parking garage used by moviegoers while attending the Jack London Cinemas on parallel Washington Street. Embarcadero Street was directly in front of her. The street was split in two by the railroad tracks. A power station loomed a block away, across from a huge crane and container loading dock still buzzing with activity at that late hour. It was difficult to tell which way the young woman would go once she decided to give up her game. Dora dialed Justin's number, but before she had a chance to talk with him, she saw the Mustang's brake lights flash. "Jack London Cinemas, Embarcadero, Cost Plus," she said quickly, hoping that Justin could hear her at the other end. The Mustang had begun to inch towards the exit. It stopped, veering slightly left. Dora got ready to make a U-turn.

"Damn!" Dora exclaimed as she saw Oz's van cruise down Embarcadero. He stopped, then quickly backed up. He had caught up with them. Serena zipped out of the parking lot. Dora moved to block Oz and braced for the impact. Oz swerved and missed her. By the time Dora completed the maneuver, Serena, with Oz at her heels, had turned right. Dora raced to the corner and caught sight of the van turning right again a block away onto Washington Street. She sped up, but had to slam on her brakes to let some pedestrians cross the street. A large group of moviegoers jaywalked to the parking structure across from the cinemas.

The Mustang and the Dodge van plowed through the crowded street. Serena finally stopped when a group of incensed teenage boys surrounded the Mustang and Dodge van and began to bang on both vehicles. Serena got out of her car and began to quarrel with her assailants, punching one on the face.

Dora undid her seatbelt and opened her car door to get out. But Oz had already darted out of his van, pistol in hand. Moviegoers scattered in all directions when someone shouted, "He's got a gun."

Dora saw Oz grab Serena and drag her to his van. He shoved her into it. With his door still open, Oz quickly maneuvered around the Mustang.

Dora heard a train whistle break the silence. The more distant whistle of a second train followed. Bells rang. The rail guards flashed red as they descended to block traffic. In dismay, she watched Oz's van speed up. It rammed the rail guards. Sparks flew in all directions. The van raced across the tracks, seconds before the Amtrak locomotive showed its huge nose.

Dora heard the screech of metal against metal. The train came to a complete stop, blocking view and passage. She hurried back to her car and pulled into the parking lot all the way to the fourth level. She remembered there was a walkway connecting the fourth level with the building on the other side of Embarcadero. She would have a clear view in all directions from there. She got her flashlight, made sure she still had her wallet in her pocket, her gun still in its holster, secured her car, and ran to the walkway.

"They didn't make it." Dora looked down at the crowd gathered around Oz's van. Smoke rose from it. Yellow lights flashed. Probably an Oakland police patrol, she thought, since the police department was only a few blocks away. She heard the wailing of an ambulance and saw a fire truck approach the crash. She ran across the walkway, took the elevator down to ground level, and rushed to the scene. She worked her way through to the front of the crowd. Oz's van had been hit on the rear passenger side. It lay on the driver's side leaning on a huge stone flower planter. She tried to get closer to the vehicle, but she was ordered back by a motor cop.

"But you . . . stay put. We need your statement," the cop said to a man standing next to Dora.

"What happened here?" Dora asked the man.

"A crazy driver. Me and my buddy, we couldn't believe our eyes. He must've seen the train coming and still tried to beat it."

"Are . . . Is the driver dead?"

"Would you believe it? He was coughing and bleeding, but he crawled out on his own. Then he went back in. Me and my buddy, we thought he was crazy going back in, with the smell of gas all around. Then we saw he was trying to get someone else out. A young lady. Me and my buddy, we helped him. She wasn't so lucky. Her face was all bloody. We thought she was dead. But we carried her to the sidewalk. She moaned, see? Then she went wild, jerking and trying to get up.

We had to restrain her. Just then the van caught on fire and we had to carry her away. I ran to Tony Roma's, the restaurant there. I got an extinguisher. We got busy trying to put out the fire as best we could, but we had to give up and just keep back. Then we went to check on the young lady."

"What happened to the driver?"

"He disappeared. So did the girl. See that woman there?" the man asked, pointing at a silver-haired woman a few feet away from them. "That lady says she doesn't know where the driver went, but she saw the young lady get up. She tried to stop her, but the girl, hurt as she was, pushed her so hard the lady went down."

"Where could she be?" Dora asked.

"Can't tell you that. All I know's she ran in that direction." The man pointed at the power station down Embarcadero.

Time to call in the cavalry. Dora punched in Justin's phone number. She briefed him on the situation and described the area where Serena was supposed to be. She rushed on foot down Embarcadero, past the Cost Plus store to the power station.

She could see the second train, which she had heard before, still waiting. It blew its whistle. She turned her flashlight on. The crane and container loading area were well lighted, but light hardly spilled from it to the area she traversed. The pavement joined with the tracks. She clumsily made her way to the power station. She checked for any holes in the fence, but found none. There was no way Serena could have climbed over the tall fence, hurt as she was. She saw two old container cars a short distance away and headed there. They were locked. She came upon a third container car. She stepped on some cans right in front of it. She was about to check the door when it suddenly opened. Dora reached for her gun and directed her light to the dark hole.

"Watcha doin' here? Get out!" a man said. He was wearing an A's cap and ragged blue jeans and brandishing a broken bottle in the air.

Dora put her gun back in its holster. "Listen, I'm just looking for my friends. Have you seen anyone around?"

The man thrust the broken bottle in the air, as if he were a musketeer fending off a ghostly enemy.

Dora held back a giggle. "I'll make it worth your while. Ten," she offered to sweeten the pie.

"Twen'y. An' turn that light off."

"Deal," she said and lowered the beam, but did not turn off the flashlight. She reached in her pants pocket for her wallet. Luckily, she had two twenties in it. She took one out. She waved the bill in front of the light, then shone the beam on him again. The man sat on the edge of the wagon and held his hand out.

When Dora did not hand him the bill, he said, "Sure've seen your friends. Man second. Woman first. She was drunk, crawling down there. I asked her to share, but she stumbled away. Then the man came around. He stepped on my alarm." He pointed at the ground. Dora saw several cans tied together. "I peeked through a hole and saw him, but he didn' see me."

"How long ago?"

"You see me wearin' a watch? I dunno. But it was right after the whistle. She blows every fifteen minutes," he said, directing her attention to the locomotive far away.

"Did you see which way the woman went?"

"She wen' that way." He pointed again in the direction of the waiting train.

Dora handed him the bill. He went back in the car and slammed the door shut.

Dora aimed her flashlight at the ground. There were many shoe prints. She noticed that some of them were actually footprints, a single bare foot, followed by a small shoe print. Serena had probably lost a shoe or slipper in the crash. Dora hoped she was right and not just wasting precious time as she followed the footprints around the homeless man's container.

She thought she heard a noise behind her. She turned her light off and listened intently. It sounded as if a cat was scratching a screen door, and its echo was being carried by the evening breeze. But the crunching sound on the opposite side sent her heart on a skip and jump. Someone had just stepped on the old man's can alarm. She took her gun out. Mashed against the container car, she moved slowly until she could sneak a look at the area around its door. Vacant. She waited. Silence. Then she leaped out of her hiding place, gun in hand, ready to fire. No one there. She rested her head against the metal to catch her breath. The train whistled and began to move slowly down the tracks. Her heart jumped in her chest. The single powerful train beam shed light on a figure dressed in blue, staggering down the tracks towards the locomotive. Serena. She wanted to shout a warning, but with someone else, possibly Oz, close by, she decided against it. She racked her brain for a possible plan but saw no alternative. She was getting ready to run across the tracks when she felt the warmth of a hand on her shoulder. Something pressed over her mouth. She froze. Her head crammed with possible escape scenarios. None feasible.

"Shh. It's me, Justin. Back up slowly. Oz is on the other side of the car."

Dora let out a sigh of relief. "Serena . . ." she whispered.

"Yes, I saw her. You'll have to get past him. On the count of three, zigzag across the tracks, fast as you can. He'll have to come out of hiding. Leave the rest to me."

"Bait for a fed. Thanks for the help, partner," Dora said. She took a deep breath.

Justin counted. Dora screamed and bolted out. Oz stepped out in the open. Two gunshots cracked the silence but missed Dora, who was clear of the tracks and still running.

"Oz," Justin said at the top of his lungs. "Give it up."

"No way, man," Oz responded.

Justin saw the shadow move. Oz spread his legs apart, like an Old West gunslinger. He fired. Justin lunged to the side and fired at the shadow.

Justin felt the sting of the bullet as it went through his left shoulder. He felt the warmth of his blood, rushing down his arm. He aimed his weapon again and fired. The shadow fell to the ground. He tried to ignore the pain now zigzagging from shoulder to hand. He crawled the distance to the spot where he had seen Oz go down.

Oz was lying spread-eagle on the ground. He was not moving.

Justin struggled to stand up as he held his injured arm. He shoved Oz's gun out of reach with his shoe and looked in the direction of the moving train. Dora was closer to Serena now, but so was the train.

Oz coughed. Justin knelt beside him. "Don't talk." He wiggled his cell phone out of his pocket, dialed nine-one-one, and asked for an ambulance.

"Get the bastard. Make Pretty Boy pay." A long sigh wheezed out of Oz's mouth.

Justin felt for his pulse. The old fed was gone. Justin got up and stumbled across the tracks.

Serena lay on the tracks, seemingly lifeless. Dora raced toward her, the train speeding toward both of them. Nothing else was on Dora's mind but winning that race. She did not falter on her purpose, not even when two bullets whizzed past her, or when she heard the thundering of three other gunshots.

Already at the spot, she had no time to feel for Serena's pulse. She grabbed her by the armpits and began to drag her away. She had almost managed to get them both out of harm's way, but Serena's blue robe got caught on something. Dora felt around for whatever was pinning the garment down. She followed the twist of the fabric to a spike. The material was sheer enough, but Dora still had a hard time tearing into it. So she began to slide the young woman out of the gown. A halo of light around them narrowed, then began to expand again. The jangling of the railcars grew louder but not more frequent. Dora heard the jarring of metal wheels against rails. The train engineer had probably seen them and had pulled the brakes, Dora hoped. But would the giant iron horse stop in time?

"Work it. Work it," Dora kept repeating to herself. Serena was finally free of her gown. Dora turned her over and rolled her over the tracks, then lunged forward with all the might she could muster up. She hit ground. The engine whizzed past them.

Dora was not sure where she was hurt. Her whole body felt numb. She made sure nothing was broken before attempting to get up. She managed to stand up, but her wobbly legs gave way, and she fell to the ground again. She crawled to where Serena lay. She found her pulse, faint but present. She put her ear to Serena's chest, to make sure. But all Dora could hear was her own blood pounding wildly against her temples. She lay face up on the ground next to Serena and stared at the moon, high in the sky. She followed the contouring stars of the Little Dipper to the dim North Star—the jingle bell on the baby bear's tail, as her father had shown her . . . ages and galaxies ago. As long as she could see the stars, she would be all right, she told herself. She began to repeat her name mentally, as though she were a little girl again, afraid that she might not know what to do if she got lost.

TWENTY-ONE
Intimations of Mortality

JUSTIN WOKE UP TO THE BEEPING of a heart monitor. A nurse greeted him with a smile and a "nice to have you back." He heard the beeping of the monitor speed up. All at once, he recalled the events of the night before. He had killed Oz.

He tried to get up, but the wound in his shoulder reminded him of his own mortality. The physician in charge walked in as the nurse advised Justin to lie back. He informed Justin that the bullet the surgeon had removed had perforated his shoulder. The soft tissues had been only slightly damaged. Unfortunately, the bullet had nicked an artery, a bleeder, but Justin was going to be all right. The cops had been around, asking when they could talk to him. They would have to wait a while longer, the doctor told Justin before he left.

The nurse injected a sedative into his IV line. He needed his rest, she told him. He wanted to ask her about Dora and Serena. But he knew the nurse would not be able to answer his questions. After she left, he looked for a phone to call Gloria, tell her what happened, ask her to come back. But there was no phone in the room. He looked at the beam of light, wedged in the slit between the drawn curtains. It crept up on his chest until it reached his pupils, blinding him for an instant. He closed his eyes and was suddenly aware of the vast sinkhole in his mind.

He opened his eyes again hours later. Dora was there, sitting on a chair, reading a book.

"Hey, partner," she greeted him. "How're you feeling?"

"Not bad, considering," Justin answered. "How did you manage to get in to see me?"

"I told the nurse I was your lawyer. Nice woman. She winked and let me in."

He cracked a smile and said, "Would you do me a favor and call Gloria? There's no phone here, as you can see."

"Already did. She's driving down from the mountains as we speak."

Anticipating all his other questions, Dora summarized the events of the night before. So far the police had no reason to doubt his shooting Oz qualified as self-defense. Fair and square. There were no charges pending against him or herself. Serena had sustained fractures of ribs, cheeks, and nose. Her face was a mess. She was in serious but stable condition in the ICU at Kaiser, where TV and newspaper reporters were already in line to interview the Saucedos. Reluctantly, Dora had had to surrender Oz's files and journal to the cops, so they would allow her to travel to Denver. She had reservations for a flight early that evening.

"Saucedo told me he'll take care of your expenses. He gave me a check for two thousand dollars. How do you like them apples?" Dora said.

"He should have given you more. The least he can do for you. You saved Serena's life." Looking at the book in her hand, he asked, "I see you're reading about the Crusade for Justice."

"Yeah. Thanks for the books. I spent the night at OPD. Thank God the cops let me get my car out of the Jack London parking lot. I had the books there. So I took them with me. Reading saved me from going bonkers. You know how it is." She patted Justin's hand. "The cops are going to be here any minute, I'm sure. I'd better mosey on. Let you rest. I need to get some sleep, too."

"You might not need his help, but call Luis Móntez, anyway, and let him know you're coming."

Justin began to tell her about Móntez. Dora told him it was not necessary, but Justin insisted. She took her notepad out and jotted down bits of information about Móntez.

A nurse came into the room and announced that two police detectives were on their way up.

"Take care, partner," Dora said, already at the door. "I'll call Gloria from Denver, if I get a chance."

Justin tried to gather his thoughts together, but his mind refused to rehearse what he would tell the cops. He would wait for their questions. All he wanted at the moment was to see Gloria's face, hear her say that she loved him, that everything was going to be all right. He would ask her to marry him. Many times during their long relationship, he had toyed with the idea, but it had not seemed right. Fear she might say no, fear she might say yes. It did not matter. This time, it felt right. He was smiling when he heard the knock on his door.

TWENTY-TWO
Mile High Blues

DORA ALWAYS FOUND AIRPORTS exhilarating. Traveling was one of her passions in life, no matter the cause or purpose for a trip. But what she hated most was having to request clearance from airport security for the gun in her luggage. It was cumbersome and time-consuming, but it beat trying to get her P.I. license back after a firearm violation.

While she waited to board her flight to Denver, she reached in her carry-on tote for a large manila envelope. She made sure she had Vincent and Jesse Latour's photos. Then she pulled out the snaps of Sheila Ray, Felicia, and Elena, Pretty Boy Patterson's three rape victims in Denver. They stared at her, young, smiling, and still trusting. She put the photos back in the envelope.

She got her notebook out and began to read her notes on Luis Móntez. She had called Móntez earlier, and he had agreed to put her in contact with people who had participated in the Chicano civil rights movement in Denver at the time of the Crusade for Justice's youth conferences. Luis was also familiar with the neighborhood around Palabras con Sabor Coffeehouse and Bookstore. She accepted his offer to pick her up at the airport. Luis's voice was pleasant, with a bit of a raspy edge, enough to make her ask herself what the man who owned that voice looked like. Justin had not described the attorney for her, but he had said that Luis was a very competent lawyer, who, as a student, had participated in the Chicano youth movement in Denver back in the sixties and seventies. His heart was in the right place, and his politics, too, although it was his heart that got him into trouble more often than not. If nothing else, she and Luis had that in common.

There she was, entangled in the thorny vines of violence and death with the end of torture nowhere in sight yet. And all because of her guilt. Her mother would be laughing, she was sure, wherever she was. But maybe, just maybe she would be praying for her, too.

Her eyes were beginning to bother her. The night before, with adrenaline still flowing and the police buzzing around, interrogating everyone involved in the case, she had hardly had any rest. She had managed to keep her wits about her by reading the two books on the Crusade for Justice.

The authors, Ernesto Vigil and Juan Haro, had both been Corky Gonzales's lieutenants. Vigil's *The Crusade for Justice* was a scholarly, well-researched history text. Haro's *Ultimate Betrayal* was a more nitty-gritty account of his years with the Crusade. Dora held in her hand one of the few available copies of Haro's book. For some undisclosed reason, the book had been pulled off the shelves shortly after its publication.

She flipped through the book, trying to remember if there was anything worth reading again. The corner of an envelope caught her attention. Large, thick, and sealed, it had her name written on it. She tore it open and found ten one-hundred-dollar bills, together with a note from Beatrice in which she explained the money was half of what they had found in Oz's safe. Dora deserved it and she was going to need it in Denver. Dora shook her head and smiled.

Passengers were already boarding, so Dora put everything back in her carry-on tote. Fifteen minutes later, she settled in her coach seat and closed her eyes, hoping to get some more rest. But all the events of the night before still haunted her. She was certain Justin would be officially cleared of all charges pertaining to Oz's death. The cops were surely picking over the bones in Oz's journal, particularly Patterson's. Maybe justice would finally be done in Pretty Boy's case, but she doubted it. She was almost sure the statute of limitations on his crimes had run out. She made up her mind to release her copies of Oz's files to the press upon her return to Oakland. Poetic justice, perhaps, but at least the man would be out of commission politically.

Would Ramona Serna ever regain consciousness? Life had not been kind to her, perhaps death would be. Dora had talked to Elizabeth briefly on her way out of Kaiser Hospital. Ramona's condition had deteriorated after her heart had gone into ventricular fibrillation. Her brain had been robbed of vital oxygen. The doctors stabilized her heart, but her brain activity had decreased considerably. Doctors at Highland doubted she would ever come out of the coma and had advised the Sernas to consider disconnecting their daughter's life support system. Grasping for straws, Elizabeth had confided in Ramona's father, telling him about Ramona's rape and about Irene and Gabi, his biological granddaughter and great-granddaughter. By the time she had finished, Mr. Serna was sobbing like an infant, blaming himself and his wife for abandoning Ramona when she needed them most. Now it was too late to make amends to his daughter. But he could at least let himself and his wife be tested for bone marrow compatibility. To Elizabeth's surprise, Mrs. Serna had consented to the test.

The lights were finally dimmed in the plane cabin. The din in it and the hum of the jet engines became a welcomed lullaby for Dora. Her mind escaped to a place where nothing but warm darkness existed.

An hour and a half later, somewhat rested, Dora was looking around the arrival gate, trying to spot a Chicano lawyer in his midfifties. She saw a man, arms crossed over his chest, with his foot resting on the pedestal of a vacant check-in counter. He had been furtively watching her. He made no attempt to approach her, and she waited for a while. But patience in such circumstances was not one of her virtues. So she approached the man.

"I'm Dora," she said, extending her hand. "*Mucho gusto*," she added, "I hope you haven't been waiting long."

"Not at all," the man answered, shaking her hand. A smile brightened for an instant his otherwise serious countenance. He did not, however, say his name.

He inquired about her baggage, and Dora told him she had had to check her bag. He pointed the way out of the gate with his open palm.

Was this what happened to women who disappeared without a trace? Dora wondered. Did it begin with a friendly gesture from a handsome stranger with a nice smile? Should she excuse herself after she retrieved her other bag, go into the toilet, and put her gun in her handbag?

As if to allay her fears, the man said, "I hope you don't mind, but I contacted some old friends and acquaintances on your behalf. All of them were involved in the Chicano youth movement. All participated in the Crusade's youth conferences you're interested in. Some can meet with you—us—tonight for an hour or so. If it's okay with you."

"Thanks, Mr. Móntez."

"Luis, please."

She breathed a sigh of relief.

As they got in his car, he suggested they swing by her hotel. She could check in and freshen up. Dora agreed. On the way to her hotel, Luis talked about the various parts of town they traversed. Denver was divided into quadrants—North, South, East, and West sides. The Crusade for Justice had operated from its headquarters in the Eastside, which was now a predominantly black community. Luis himself had been born and raised in the Northside, at that time an Italian neighborhood. It had later become home to Chicano families who worshiped at Our Lady of Guadalupe Church. He and Dora would be meeting his friends at the Bella Vista Lounge on 20th Street, one of his favorite hangouts. Closed for the day, Palabras con Sabor, the coffeehouse frequented by Latour, was located on 22nd Street.

Dora gave Luis a brief account of events in Oakland and reassured him that Justin was going to be all right. Then she talked briefly about the contents in Oz's safe and Patterson's criminal activities in Denver. She was sure Luis was listening, but he hardly uttered even an "Uh-huh" all the while.

"What's your take on all this?" she asked.

"I don't remember hearing about any of the women being raped at the time. But it's very possible—obviously true in the case of Patterson. A few years ago, Chicanas filed rape charges against Sydney Parker, a Denver cop back in the sixties and seventies. They claimed they'd been raped by him. But it took the women almost three decades to come forward with their accusations."

"Why was that?"

"The usual reason—fear."

"Of what? Reprisal? Public shame?"

"Probably all of the above. But there's another kind of fear. A burden for women, no doubt. When it happened, the rape victims knew that the men in their families would, let's say, take matters into their own hands."

"Kill the perps?"

"The perps," Luis repeated and laughed.

Dora chuckled nervously. "Sorry. I've been hanging out with cops, feds, and P.I.'s too long, I guess."

"No. I'm the one who should apologize. I do. At any rate, for the obvious reasons, Chicanos couldn't trust the system to deliver justice. In the case of rape, the men in the victim's family would probably take care of or take out a rapist. But Parker was a cop at a time when cops literally got away with murder. The women were afraid for their families. It's understandable they didn't come forward with such allegations at the time."

"Justin tells me you were involved in the Crusade's youth movement back then. What was it like?"

"I was directly involved in the youth movement. We all had something or another to do with the Crusade." Luis straightened up in his seat, but he added nothing to his statement. At his reaction, Dora decided to pursue the matter some other time.

Luis checked the rearview mirror twice, something Dora found intriguing as she realized that he had repeatedly done that before. She looked over her shoulder, wondering if they were being followed. From that moment on, she watched the action behind them in the side mirror. She was not able to detect anyone following the usual patterns of vehicle surveillance. Either the person tailing them was a pro, or he was only a product of her overloaded suspicious psyche.

TWENTY-THREE
The View from Bella Vista

THE BELLA VISTA LOUNGE caught Dora's immediate attention. It was an eyeful with its rich dark wood counter and carvings and huge wood-framed mirror. The bar counter offered a striking contrast to the off-white walls of the lounge. Small wall lighting fixtures provided dim illumination to the few patrons sitting at the small tables.

Luis walked ahead of her and was already greeting a group of two women and two men when Dora joined him.

Gordo, the taller of two men, was the first to introduce himself. He was slender, and Dora wondered what had earned him such a nickname. He was wearing a baseball cap with no team insignia on it. He did not offer to shake hands with her but took it upon himself to make the introductions.

The other man, Chuy, was of medium height and build. He had bright, big eyes, lined with long, straight lashes. "Smiling eyes," Dora thought as she shook his hand.

Cynthia, the oldest of the two women, was cordial and affable and immediately inquired about Dora's flight to Denver. She wore her long hair in a french twist; strands of white hair along her temples belied her youthful countenance. Cynthia introduced Dora to her daughter, Suzanne, who was perhaps in her early twenties and had inherited her mother's good looks. But the furrows in her forehead told of a rather reserved attitude. Suzanne was thrilled to be there, Cynthia explained. She was looking into various types of careers; private investigations was one of them. Perhaps later, she and Dora could talk about what it took to become a private detective.

"You're tall. But look at *m'ija*, beautiful, but so petite," Cynthia said. "I don't think she could take down a two-hundred-pound criminal."

"Neither can I. I'm a fast runner, though," Dora said. The men laughed.

Dora saw the waves of red lapping up Suzanne's cheeks. She gave the young woman a reassuring smile and remembered her mother taking inventory of Dora's minuses and pluses. She was beautiful but so-o-o tall. Her curly hair was shiny but so unruly that she should wear it short. She had nice, round, small breasts, but her butt stuck out like two large *melones*. She should always watch her weight so the cantaloupes would not turn into watermelons. But Dora had a good and quick mind, and that, in the end, was all that counted.

Dora looked at Luis when his gaze shifted to two women who had just entered the lounge. He waved at them. Dora realized she knew nothing about Luis's personal life. She turned her attention to the group and caught Chuy's smiling eyes focused on her. She smiled back.

The waiter brought two pitchers of beer and Chuy filled everyone's glasses. "*Salud*," everyone cheered.

Dora took only a sip. The gurgling in her stomach was a good indicator she needed food. She called the bar waitress back and ordered chimichangas for everyone. She also instructed the waitress to bring bar and food tabs to her.

"So. Luis here tells us that you want to know about Corky and the Crusade," Gordo said in a low voice. He threw a glance over his shoulder. "What do you want to know?" he asked as his eyes swept over the area around the group.

Luis and Cynthia, as if moved by the same string, pulled their chairs in. But not Chuy, who slid down in his chair and crossed his arms, nor Suzanne whose attention had shifted to a couple of young Chicanos walking into the Bella Vista.

Dora found herself puzzling over Gordo, Luis, and Cynthia's peculiar reaction. Were they expecting to see a cop or an FBI agent walk in and arrest them thirty years after the Crusade's heyday? Luis had behaved in a similar manner on their way from the airport.

"Actually, I'm not interested in Corky Gonzales or the Crusade, per se," Dora said.

Gordo and Cynthia relaxed in their chairs. Luis responded with a head nod.

Dora took out a penlight and the photos of Sheila Ray, Elena, and Felicia, the three young women Patterson had raped in Denver. She laid the photos on the table and shone the penlight on each of them.

"Do any of you remember these women? They're, of course, much older now. I'm trying to find them."

Gordo picked up the photos. He and Luis examined them intently. Both men shook their heads and passed each picture on to the others. Cynthia and Chuy were the last ones to look at the pictures.

"I think I met her," Cynthia said, putting her finger on Felicia's photo. "I vaguely remember her, though. I think she was from . . . Argentina? No, no. She was from Chile. Yeah. I remember we used to tease her. How could someone from Chile not eat *chile*. I think she and other women from Boulder came to talk to us, the Chicanas at North High, just before the student walkout in . . . Was it in February?" She scratched her head, trying to remember. "My mind is *masa*, corn mush, lately. Estrogen withdrawal," she said and laughed. "I'm beginning to forget even my own name."

Dora raised her eyebrows. Just how reliable the information Cynthia had just given her remained to be seen.

"It was in February. 1970. Your name is Cynthia. And you were a real *guerrillera,* a real woman warrior, back then," Chuy interjected.

"*Chale, ése.* For your information, *todavía lo soy*—I still am. You were, too. *Con tu* billy club," Cynthia answered. To Dora, she said, "Gordo was a senior at West High. Chuy and I went to North High. I was a junior. He was a senior, a Black Beret. The Black Berets challenged fascist Principal Shannon's 'no berets on campus' rule."

Dora squinted. She was trying to remember what she had read about the student walkouts in Vigil's *The Crusade for Justice.*

"You probably don't know what we're talking about," Chuy remarked.

"Actually, I think I do," Dora said. "Let me see if I got it right. You were told you couldn't wear your black berets—your colors—on campus. You protested. The school administration wouldn't back down. The Black and Brown Berets and students from other high schools staged a march to the Board of Education building. The cops were waiting for you, batons in hand. You had billy clubs, too. And you engaged in what Vigil calls the 'sword fight.'"

"All right!" Cynthia and Chuy said. Luis gave Dora an admiring look.

"Nothing to it. Actually, I just finished reading Vigil's book on the Crusade."

"One thing the Crusade did for us is it backed us up, always, no questions asked," Cynthia said. "Corky was always interested in the youth movement. He felt we were the future leaders, the . . ." Cynthia looked at Gordo and Luis, who were shaking their heads. "What? You don't agree with me?"

Arms crossed over his chest, Chuy looked at Cynthia with condescending eyes, but he remained quiet.

"We're not saying nothing, *ésa.*" Gordo raised his arms. Again, his eyes roved around the lounge, as if he were looking to spot someone eavesdropping. Luis also threw a furtive look around his periphery.

It dawned on Dora that the men were not afraid of cops or FBI agents suddenly materializing and arresting them. Until that moment, she had not quite fully understood the power Corky Gonzales had had over everyone. For Suzanne and for her, Corky, though still alive, was only a historical figure they had heard or read about.

A moment of silence ensued. Gordo looked at his watch. It was ten o'clock. He got up.

Dora saw him reach into his wallet. "It's on me," she said and thanked him. This time Gordo shook her hand as he said good-night.

No one seemed eager to resume their conversation. Dora was racking her brain for a way to steer their attention back to the photos, when Suzanne asked, "So, Mom. Did you ever see her again?" She put her finger on Felicia's photo. Dora smiled at her, grateful for her intervention.

"Yeah. I saw her again, about a year later. She was a volunteer at Escuela Tlatelolco—the Crusade's school. She tutored math. My sisters needed help with their math. She tutored them for a while. I went looking for her weeks later. I wanted to see if she could help me with my Spanish. But no one seemed to know where she was."

"Do you know her last name or if she's still in Boulder or Denver?" Dora asked.

Cynthia puckered her lips and shook her head.

"I saw her once again," Chuy said, picking up Felicia's photo.

"Once again?" Cynthia asked. *"Eres un diablo."*

Chuy smiled. "Puppy love." He chuckled. "She was beautiful. I was working evenings at a gas station 'round the corner from her apartment house, near the Crusade's building on Downing. She used to get gas there. We talked many times, about everything, nothing, just talk. But I never had the guts to ask her out. One night, I was leaving work about nine in the evening. She was walking home. It was strange because she drove everywhere in her Peugeot. I noticed she was walking barefoot, but she had only one shoe in her hand. She was weaving as she walked. *Como borrachita.* Maybe she'd been drinking. I thought of catching up to her, but I changed my mind. I followed her just to make sure she got home okay.

"To get to her apartment, she had to go through the alley in back of the Crusade building. She stopped. I stopped, too, only a few feet behind her. She was looking at something up ahead. I hid behind some bushes to take a look at the action there. I thought something was going on at the Crusade. Not this time. But Corky Gonzales was there, dressed all in black, his arms crossed over his chest. The light from a street lamp behind him bounced off his silhouette, like a halo. He stood there, alone; none of his lieutenants or the other *vatos* that were always with him were around. I wondered what was going on. Like most everyone else I knew, I'd never spoken more than a few words with Corky. I walked up to him and asked, 'Everything all right?' He nodded. I said good-night and he answered with a *'buenas.'* When I looked for Felicia, she was gone. I ran through the passageway to the other end of the street. I went to her apartment house. The light was on and I assumed she'd made it home. The next day we all woke up to the news of a bloody battle between the pigs and Crusade members, sometime after Felicia and I were there. But I got worried about her. I went to her apartment and talked with her roommate. She told me Felicia had left for Chile on a family emergency. I never saw her again."

"Do you remember her last name?" Dora asked.

Chuy frowned and lowered his eyes, intent upon remembering. "Something like Lata. It sounded like that."

"Latour," Dora suggested.

"Yeah. Something like that."

Dora took out Jesse Latour's photo and put it on the table. "Do you know him?"

Chuy and Cynthia indicated they had never seen Latour. Luis recognized the photo he had taken of Jesse Latour. Dora signaled for him to keep quiet.

"Who's he?" Chuy asked.

"I'm now pretty sure this young man is Felicia's son," she said, then laid Oz's and Patterson's photos on the table. "How about them, have you ever seen them before?"

"Nope," Cynthia and Chuy replied.

"What's all this about?"

"I'm not sure yet. I'll let you know when I finish my investigation," Dora said.

Dora's last remark reminded Cynthia that Suzanne was still interested in learning more about private investigations. Dora and Suzanne talked for a few minutes while the others listened. When they were ready to leave, Dora gave Suzanne her business card in case she had other questions later, and then she paid the tab.

Chuy was not ready to go home yet, so he ordered another beer. "Take good care of her, *carnal*," he told Luis. Pointing with his chin at Dora, he said, "I'll be seeing you." He raised his bottle of beer. The smile in his eyes was now buried underneath misty layers of alcohol vapors and bittersweet memories.

When Luis offered to take her on a night tour of the places Chuy, Cynthia, and Gordo had mentioned, Dora gladly accepted.

"You made quite an impression on Chuy. He would have never told any of us what he told you tonight." Luis looked at Dora out of the corner of his eye. "It doesn't surprise me."

"Hmm," Dora uttered and offered no other comment. If Luis wanted to probe into her feelings about anyone, including himself, he would have to ask the pertinent questions. She suspected he would not. His silence proved her right.

History was a much safer ground for him, she supposed, as he drove them around the downtown and Westside areas, focusing on the sites of many protest marches, rallies, and riots that had taken place in the late sixties and early seventies. The brief tour included a ride by the Escuela Tlatelolco, the alternative school established by the Crusade. It was run then as now by Corky Gonzales's family. It was also one of the last places where Felicia Latour did volunteer work.

The tour ended at the site of what had once been the Crusade for Justice headquarters and apartment buildings, purchased by the Crusade in the seventies. In his book, Juan Haro had mentioned that many Crusade families had contributed or loaned money toward the purchase of the property. The Gonzales family had sold the property to the federal government for nearly a million dollars in the eighties. The old buildings had been demolished and a U.S. Postal Service station had been erected in its place.

Luis parked in the alley behind the post office. He waited in the car while Dora got out and walked around, trying to reenact in her mind the details Chuy had supplied her earlier. Disheveled and obviously in distress, Felicia Latour had stood there so many years before. Holding one shoe in her hand, she had watched Corky Gonzales as he stood there, alone, light bouncing off his figure like a halo, taller than the tallest Chicano tall tale.

Back in the car, Dora asked, "Is it true what Haro says in his book, that Corky and his family shouldn't have sold the property because it wasn't theirs to sell?"

Taken by surprise, Luis looked at her first, then his eyes swept the perimeter around the car.

Unable to hold her curiosity any longer, Dora remarked, "Every time we talk about the Crusade, you and Gordo look over your shoulders. Who do you really expect to see, a cop, a fed, or Corky?"

"I . . . Did I do that?" Luis started the car.

"You certainly did, just now and before, too."

"It's just a habit acquired years ago." He chuckled.

"Is Corky still that powerful in Denver that all of you are still terrified of what he might do if you talk ill of him or the Crusade?"

"Terrified!" Luis was angry.

Oh, dear, Dora thought. A soft-spoken and patient man, and she had tried his goodwill. Still, his reaction surprised her. She realized that her comments had rubbed the edges of a wound in him that still bled at the slightest touch.

"I'm sorry. I had no idea how deeply hurt all of you were, still are."

Luis's tone had softened considerably as he said, "Not the way you think. Many, maybe all of us, paid a high price for doing what we thought was just and right. Gladly, believe me. I can't speak for others, but personally I have no regrets. We all had our quarrels with Corky. But we set those aside and joined forces with the Crusade when necessary, too. It worked. That's all that matters."

"Haro and others don't agree with your point of view."

"A subject better left alone," Luis said, closing the door to further probing.

They rode in silence until they reached Dora's hotel.

Before Dora got out, Luis said, "I have to meet with a client and file some papers in court early tomorrow morning. From what you told me, Latour is not an early riser. Okay with you if we meet at Palabras con Sabor around eleven?"

Dora wanted to tell him it was not necessary for him to get further involved in her case. But she felt anything she said at that moment could be misconstrued as a pretext not to see him again. So she accepted his offer. Following an impulse, she leaned forward and kissed him on his cheek. She stepped out of the car, closed the door, and walked toward the hotel entrance without looking back.

TWENTY-FOUR
Words and Flurries

"I SHOULDN'T HAVE HAD those last two beers," Dora said under her breath as soon as she woke up. Her nostrils felt dry. Her head ached. She made a cup of coffee in the tiny coffeemaker in her room. It was no industrial-strength Mocha Java, but even that minute amount of caffeine got her heart going, and it somewhat alleviated her sinus headache.

After showering and getting dressed, she drew the curtains and looked out. The sun struggled with the clouds to shine on the Mile-High City. The guidebook she had read said that the sun shone in Denver three hundred days a year. She had the misfortune of being in Denver on one of the other sixty-five.

She turned the television on and searched for the weather channel. If the forecaster was right, by late evening snow would begin to fall. She hated snow. It had a way of bringing back painful memories of her mother frozen to death in the Sierra Nevada. If she located Jesse Latour early enough, if he led her to Vincent's hideaway, she would be able to leave Denver ahead of snowfall and morbid memories.

She reached for her strong hiking shoes and put them on. Bending over to lace them made her head pound again. She decided to walk downstairs and have more coffee and some juice in the lobby. After two cups, she realized her headache was not going to surrender without a fight. She reached into her handbag for a small vial of aspirin and popped a tablet into her mouth. She still had two hours to kill before she headed to the coffeehouse. She asked the reception clerk to call a taxi for her.

The taxi driver was pleasant and seemed well informed about activities around town. She asked him to drop her off at a restaurant of his choice, but in the vicinity of the coffeehouse, so she could have breakfast.

Anxiety was beginning to creep in, but the ride through the streets of Denver seemed to soothe her nerves. Denver was quite different from Oakland and San Francisco. The most obvious differences were the rust-colored brick architecture and the city's ethnic composition— some Asian Americans, a few more African Americans, many Chicanos and Latinos, but mostly people of European descent. Through its one-hundred-seventy-year history, the city had changed from a Spanish fur trading post to a gold and silver mining settlement, then a cow town, and finally a modern corporate oil and coal center. But it was Denver's American frontier town atmosphere, the guidebook had said, that had inspired Jack Kerouac to describe it as a place where he had experienced a "most wicked kind of joy" in the company of the "bums and beat cowboys of Larimer Street."

All of that was gone, yuppified, the taxi driver informed her, when she inquired about that part of town. He dropped her off at a small restaurant a few blocks away from the coffeehouse.

Breakfast was nothing to write home about, but her headache was completely gone. A brisk walk down to Palabras con Sabor cleared her mind of any debris still left from the frantic and tragic events of the last few days.

She stopped when she caught sight of the blue awning of Palabras con Sabor. The coffeehouse, together with the office of the *El Semanario* newspaper and an Autobuses de México/Ace Express bus ticket office at the corner, occupied the ground floor of a red brick building. The second story probably housed apartments, judging from the potted plants and the wrought iron work adorning and protecting the windows from unwelcome visitors.

Behind her and directly across from the coffeehouse building were two large parking lots. The lots were separated by a passageway, which ran their length and continued on past the street there. At the other end of the parking lots rose long one-story buildings that looked like warehouses. The entrance to the warehouses faced the passageway, not the main street. Beyond the warehouses, high-rise buildings fenced the area in on two sides.

There was quite a bit of activity at the warehouses, which seemed to temporarily cease when two Denver police cars cruised down the side street, turned at the corner, and entered the parking lot directly across from the coffeehouse. The activity at the warehouses resumed. Dora responded to the officers' morning greeting with a smile and turned her attention back to her surroundings.

To her left, the same narrow alley running the length of the parking lots also separated the coffeehouse building from another one-story brick building and a car wash. The car wash walls were painted Mexican pink, with the woodwork in turquoise; a narrow, white-lined, black serpentine road coursed the walls all around. Various signs announced the price for the wash; arrows pointed to the exit. Other signs advised the customers to use the rear entrance for access into the car wash.

A white Ford Crown Victoria parked in front of the coffeehouse. Two men got out. They were wearing civilian clothes, but Dora suspected they were either federal agents or plainclothes detectives. They entered the coffeehouse.

Dora walked in right behind them. She realized they were regulars when she saw the young women at the counter greet them in a familiar way. She ordered a latte. It felt hot inside the coffeehouse, so she went outside.

A man came out, coffee cup and a pack of cigarettes in hand. He was a chatty fellow and soon had engaged her in small talk.

"What's in those buildings?" she asked, pointing at the high-rises behind the warehouses.

"Federal offices," the man said.

"That explains why so many cops and agents come here to get their daily brew. There is a lot of activity in the warehouses, too," Dora remarked. "I wonder what goes on in there."

"Cops suspect there may be a chop shop in one of them. They've raided the place, but so far they haven't found enough evidence to shut it down." His cigarette finished, the man walked back in.

Dora decided to stay outside. She wanted to take a look at Jesse

Latour as he made his way to the coffeehouse. Fifteen minutes later, she spotted a redheaded man turn the corner and walk into the Autobuses de México/Ace Express office. He looked clean-shaven, unlike the man in the photo that Luis Móntez had sent. Dora looked at her watch. It was ten-thirty.

A few minutes later, Jesse Latour came out of the Ace Express office, carrying a boxed parcel. Dora guessed that he either had a mailbox there or got packages shipped to the Ace Express. If so, he had to live somewhere in the vicinity. She thought it best to tail him, find out more about him. Perhaps he would lead her to Vincent Constantino.

When the redhead was near the door, Dora began to walk toward it as well. She looked at his face. The man was Latour, all right. Wiry and stealthy, he was shorter and slimmer than she had anticipated. Something to be thankful for, she thought. He saw her. She smiled at him. He did not return the greeting but held the door open for her to go in. His hair looked damp, and he smelled strongly of aftershave, both strong indicators that he lived someplace nearby.

Latour stopped at the door and picked up a copy of *El Semanario*, printed every week next door. She snuck a look at the headlines and wondered why a paper aimed at Latinos was in English, but it was. Dora assumed that perhaps Latour's reading skills surpassed his oral command of English. Or perhaps he just wanted to blend in.

She spotted an empty table next to the window in the bookstore's reading room, not far from the front door. Someone had left an open book on the table—*Erased Faces,* by Graciela Limón. She opened the book and began to read it, furtively looking in Latour's direction from time to time.

Seemingly relaxed, Latour walked to the coffee counter and ordered his daily favorite. Dora saw him smile as he glanced at a poster advertising the sale of bagged beans of "Zapatista Coffee from Chiapas." She tried to ascertain if he packed a pistol, but, warm as it was inside the coffeehouse, Latour never took off his parka.

He put his parcel down on the floor and settled into one of the easy chairs in the reading room, sipped his coffee, and proceeded to leaf through the newspaper. Twenty minutes later, he folded the paper, drained the last drop of coffee, picked up his parcel, and got up.

Dora gathered her handbag and pushed her chair back. When Latour made his way to the door, she got up and headed slowly to the exit. By the time she was out the door, Latour had already crossed the alleyway between the coffeehouse and the car wash. He reached the corner and turned. She rushed to the spot and snuck a look before turning the corner. Latour was talking to a man wearing a black cap and blazer. He kept tapping the box in his hand with his index finger. With his back to her, the other man blocked Latour's view of her.

Dora turned the corner and strolled down the street. Latour became aware of her presence and looked in her direction. The other man turned to look at her.

"Gotcha," she muttered to herself as she recognized Vincent Constantino. She tried to hush her inner voice, warning her that nothing in her business was ever that easy.

She approached them. The men moved out of the way and leaned on the pink wall.

"I need directions," she said. "Someone told me there's a car paint shop around here. But I haven't been able to find it. Would you happen to know where it is?"

"I don't know of any," Constantino said, frowning but seemingly undisturbed. Looking at Latour, he asked, "*¿Tú sabes de un* car paint *por aquí?*"

Latour squinted and shook his head. He pressed the parcel to his stomach and eyed Dora as if trying to remember something. Dora sensed she had aroused his suspicion. But how? He'd never laid eyes on her, except outside the coffeehouse. They had only talked on the phone twice. She cursed inwardly. He might have recognized her voice. She should have thought of it before she had gone on babbling about some car paint shop.

Latour stepped sideways. He looked at Vincent. Before Dora could come up with something else, he shouted, "Run! *Ésta es la que te anda buscando para matarte.* She keel you, man."

"Wait! I'm not trying to kill you," she shouted. Too late.

Constantino and Latour ran to the corner and turned. She rushed after them. When she reached the car wash area, she saw them moving as fast as they could down the narrow space between cars and wall. She stepped up her pace. They ran out and crossed the street to the parking lot, where only one of the Denver police cars was still parked.

Dora spotted Luis's car coming down the street. She waved at him, but did not stop. She ran past the patrol. The Chicano cop she had seen earlier was sitting in it. She heard the patrol car start up almost immediately after she went past it. She threw a quick glance back and saw it back out of the parking lot. Farther down, Luis was fast moving on foot toward the warehouses.

Latour ran faster than Vincent. A good thing. Dora prayed that Vincent would not get to the warehouses, where she would surely lose him or the Chicano cop would catch up to him.

Dora was already crossing the street when she saw Latour run down the passageway and enter one of the warehouses. Having apparently caught a second wind, Vincent was only a few steps behind Latour.

The patrol car approached fast and came to a halt as Dora got to the entrance. She snuck a look. It was an auto body shop. She did not see anyone there. Then, suddenly, two men in coveralls sprinted out of the place. "*¡Vete de aquí!* Don't go in there, lady!" the men yelled. They ran down the alley towards the high-rise buildings. The lights went out inside the shop.

The cop was getting out of his car and already yelling the customary warning to stop. She felt totally unprotected. But, with a cop there, she could not risk taking her gun out.

"I'm a licensed private investigator from California," she yelled back. Her words drowned in a rattling noise. The rolling metal curtain of the shop was being lowered. She had no option but to drop to the ground and crawl in. She thought she had cleared the curtain, but the weight on her left foot told a different story. She was pinned face down on the ground. She tried to turn so she could untie her hiking shoe and slide her foot out. Pain shot up her leg and thigh, warning of further injury to her ankle and hip. She looked around for something long enough to use as leverage to raise the curtain. A two-by-four next to the tall trash bin was not long enough. To her left, next to the bin was a three-foot-high stack of old batteries. She was grateful that at least from that side she was sheltered from view and gunfire.

Dora was helpless. So why had Latour not made his move? Maybe there was another way out of the shop. The two men could be long gone. But Dora could see only two small windows. In the dim light trickling in through them, she was able to make out a number of cars at various stages of dismantling. She raised herself slowly on her elbows and turned her head. She located two switches next to the curtain door—one of them, surely, the switch to raise the metal curtain, but just as surely, she could not reach it. She listened intently for any noise or footsteps. She heard only the whirring of the stuck iron curtain mechanism.

Her efforts to free her foot had left her almost breathless. Her heartbeat thundered in her ears. She took a deep breath and painfully held it in, then exhaled as much of it as she could. Taking a second breath, in a loud voice, she said, "Vincent. I'm a private investigator from Oakland. Your sister Beatrice hired me to find you." Whispering voices followed. Then silence again. She reached for her handbag and took her gun out. "Beatrice is worried about you. We know all about Patterson. Ramona Serna is in a coma at the hospital in Oakland," she added. More muted voices. Her ear followed the stream of whispers. They seemed to flow out of a car hoist trench about fifteen feet from where she was. A Camaro sat partly raised over the trench.

Dora heard a soft rap on the metal curtain, then Luis's voice asking if she was all right in there. She quickly answered with a low "Yes." Another man's voice—probably the cop—suggested using a car jack to raise the curtain enough for her to free her foot. A few grunts followed, then the sound of the jack being positioned and pumped underneath the curtain. Just in time, she thought, as she caught a glimpse of someone's shoes moving about and out of range.

Her foot and part of her leg were already numb. She was grateful for the numbness on her foot and limb, but she was afraid she would not feel the pressure off her foot when the curtain lifted. Despite the stress on her knee and hip, she kept trying to pull her shoe out. The curtain rose, and her foot was finally freed. Suddenly, the curtain crashed onto the floor. Her numb foot and leg started to become painfully alive again.

She heard footsteps and checked the trench area. No action there. But she saw the silhouette of two heads rising over the top of a tool cart about ten feet from her. Her hiding place behind the stack of batteries was no longer safe. Ignoring the pain shooting up from her injured foot, she crawled to a darker spot on the other side of the curtain and hid behind some empty cardboard boxes there. She wiped away the tears caused by the sharp pain in her ankle.

She heard sirens blare outside the body shop. The cop had called for backup, she surmised. Just then, she saw the top of Latour's head above the stack of batteries. She kept her gun pointed at him as he slowly moved alongside the stack.

Latour stood up and jumped out, pistol in hand. He lowered his gun when he saw no one was there. He took a few steps back, then turned. Despite her injury, Dora rushed towards him from his blind side and tackled him from behind. He resisted the fall but finally tumbled down to the floor, his arms spread out, but he still held the gun in his hand. She quickly rolled onto his back, pinning both his shoulders to the ground with her knees.

Dora pressed her gun, safety still on, against Latour's head. "Let go . . . *suelta la pistola*," she commanded. "*Aviéntala lejos.* C'mon, push it away!"

Latour did as told, but instead of pushing the gun away, he sent it sliding in the direction of the stack of batteries. Dora knew Vincent was there and could easily pick up the gun.

"Vincent," she called out. "I am a private detective. Your sister is my neighbor. She did hire me to find you."

"*No le creas*, man. She keel you," Latour said.

An instant later, Dora saw Vincent peer over the stack. He walked around it and came into Dora's view. He stood frozen in place, staring at her. Latour squirmed underneath her and she pressed harder on him, infuriating her already distressed ankle.

With her free hand, she took her P.I. wallet out of her coat pocket and threw it in Vincent's direction. "Look for yourself," she said. The wallet landed a few feet from Latour's gun. Dora cursed inwardly. She was relieved when Vincent picked up only the wallet and raised it to eye level. He looked at her.

She turned her attention to Vincent for a second, but when she looked down at Latour again, he had stretched his arms in front of him. With elbows bent and palms on the ground, he pushed back against her. He brought his knees up and pushed back harder. She rolled over to the side and tried to get on her feet quickly. He grabbed one of her legs and she screamed in pain. He dragged her down. She fell backwards with him on top of her legs. Tears welled up in her eyes, and she clenched her teeth to keep them from running freely. She raised her fist and hit Latour's face with it. She managed to land a second blow to his temple with the gun in her other hand. Latour cursed and reached out, trying to snatch the gun away from her. She quickly threw it over her torso as far as she could. Latour grabbed one of her arms and crawled up her belly. She gasped for breath, but kept swinging with her free arm, hitting his ear with her fist. She felt his grip on her other hand ease off. She slid her palm under his chin and pushed his head back with all her might. Latour released her other wrist and reached for her neck with one hand. She got hold of his nose and twisted it several times. Latour threw his head back and clutched her hand. She drew her free arm back and rammed his jaw with the butt of her hand repeatedly. He clutched her wrist and began to force her arm down. His face was now very close to hers. She raised her head, opened her mouth, caught his chin, and clenched her teeth hard around it. Latour screamed and let go of her hand.

Dora was ready to ram her fist into Latour's face again when she heard Vincent say, "*¡Basta!* Enough!"

She and Latour looked at Vincent. He stood right above them, holding her gun with trembling hands.

"*¡Dame la pistola!*" Latour yelled.

"None of that," Vincent answered. "No more. *No más.*" His voice quavered but the look in his eyes told a different story.

Dora got onto her feet as best she could, trying to put little pressure on her injured foot and ankle. Latour sat up on the floor. Vincent began to step back until he was right next to the curtain.

"Move to the door. *A la puerta*," Vincent said and motioned with the gun. Reaching up, he pushed both switches on the wall. The curtain started to rise. He put his gun on the floor where the cops could see it easily, and raised his arms. Dora and Latour, up on their feet, followed his lead.

"Everything is all right," Dora shouted as the curtain rose. She shivered when daylight hit her pupils. The cold wind rushed in and found its way through her clothes, dampened by her own sweat.

Armed officers rushed in as soon as the curtain was halfway up. A flurry of activity ensued. But all Dora could or wanted to see at that moment was Luis Móntez's bright smile.

TWENTY-FIVE
Fate's Victim

FINE POWDERY SNOW had begun to fall by the time the cops took Dora and Vincent's statements. They had initially questioned both of them and seemed satisfied with Dora's statement. She emphasized a few times Vincent's intervention on her behalf. But she also told them that Latour had acted in self-defense since he had no idea who she was or if she meant him harm. She suggested that they get in touch with the Oakland Police Department for further information. It was the least she could do for Latour, who, like Ramona Serna, was fate's victim all around.

The police had given relative credence to her statements. They, however, seemed more interested in Latour's activities in Denver. Officer Cedilla, the Chicano cop who had helped raise the curtain at the auto shop earlier, had asked her if she knew something about some "communiqués from guerrilla groups in Mexico." The police had found and confiscated a box of subversive materials addressed to Latour in the hoist trench. In all sincerity, she denied knowing anything about the contents of the box. She wondered if Vincent could do the same.

Vincent heard about the communiqués and became very agitated. He had refused to talk to her or anyone else about his business with Latour or with Ramona M. Serna.

Dora had taken her shoe off while they waited at the police station. The swelling around her ankle was not as bad as she had expected and, despite the pain, she kept massaging the area to restore circulation as soon as possible.

Seeing her swollen ankle, Vincent offered an apology.

Dora used the opportunity to ask him about Latour. "What's your role in all this? I'm almost positive Latour is Felicia's child. How did you find out?"

Vincent ignored her questions. Dora tried to reassure him that what he said to her would be held in her strictest confidence. Vincent still held his tongue.

Luis Móntez had left a while earlier to take care of some important business at his office. Dora suggested that Vincent ask Luis for the name of a good attorney upon his return. "I have about seven hundred dollars your sister gave me for you. Use the money as a retainer."

Vincent behaved as if he had no idea what she was talking about. Frustrated, Dora took out her cell phone and punched in Beatrice's number in Oakland. "You can at least tell your sister you're alive. You owe her that much." She handed Vincent the receiver as soon as she heard Beatrice's voice. She picked up her sock and shoe and hobbled to a window nearby to give him some privacy. She leaned against the sill and lifted her leg to rotate her stiff ankle a bit.

Vincent joined Dora at the window a few minutes later. There was moisture around his eyes.

"I'm really sorry I put Bea through all this. Of all the people in the world. . . . She's always so emotionally fragile. I didn't want to upset her."

"She's stronger than you give her credit for." Dora patted his shoulder. "And you're all the family she has. Think about that—whatever your decision."

"I'll tell you all you want to know," Vincent said after a pause.

"Good. Let's begin with Ramona. How did you meet her? And how did you end up with Willie Oz's safe?"

"I'd been doing research for an article I was writing on Third World militant organizations of the sixties in the Bay Area—Black Panthers, Third World Liberation Front, strikes at San Francisco State and Berkeley, etc. A mutual acquaintance, a writer, referred me to Ramona. As a writer who participated in the Third World Student Strike at Berkeley, she'd be able to offer a different take on it—a writer's insights. I met with her a few times, talked, but she seemed always to be holding back. She'd only give me facts that I could've read in newspapers and other publications of the time. Also, she was so drunk sometimes that she made no sense. I didn't think there was much point in meeting with her any longer.

"A couple of months after our last meeting, she called me to ask if I would be interested in writing her life story. She was sober and lucid then. I asked why she wouldn't do it herself. She was mostly a poet, she told me. Also, she said it would be too painful for her. Her request didn't seem out of the ordinary. And the idea intrigued me. Maybe she'd give me the inside dope. With some reservations, I agreed to do it. We talked many times. She had great concerns about other innocent people who would be hurt, and she couldn't offer any solid proof that what had happened to her was true. So I suggested a fictionalized story, but first-person narrative. The voice is much more compelling, more intimate, and people tend to sympathize and identify with the character a lot more. At any rate, I started work on it.

"One day, she phoned me and said that she was ready to supply the proof we needed. The next day, she called again and gave me an address and asked that I meet her there. I had no idea what was going on. When I got there, she showed me a safe. She asked me to help her carry it to her car. I hadn't the slightest idea that she had broken into that apartment. She followed me to my house so we could look at the contents of the safe. She was all excited. She told me the safe belonged to a Willie Oz."

"How had she found out that Willie Oz was in Oakland? It seems strange, doesn't it?"

"Yes, it does. What she told me was that she'd seen Willie on the street a few weeks earlier."

"Quite a coincidence, don't you think?" Dora asked.

Vincent shrugged and shook his head.

"Anyway, go on."

"Apparently, Oz didn't even recognize her. She took that as a sign of his total disregard for her. How could he forget her or what he'd done to her, she told me. She was furious. She decided right then and there to tail him, find out where he lived, get her revenge somehow. What she intended to do when she broke into his apartment was to destroy as many of his prized possessions as possible. He deserved as much punishment as she could inflict on him. At some point, she must have changed her mind. Maybe just breaking a few things and disturbing his life might not have seemed like enough. I really can't tell you. The fact is that she rummaged through his things and found the safe behind a suitcase in his closet. She went through all of his desk and chest drawers. She found a memo book with numbers that looked like bank account numbers and dates. She also found an envelope with a key and what looked like a safe combination. She decided to take the safe and envelope with her. But it proved to be too big a task. The safe was too heavy. That's when she called me. If I'd known what was going on, I wouldn't have gone there.

"At my house, she ranted and raved as we read all the documents in the safe. You see, Willie Oz didn't even mention her name. She was outraged. She left the safe in my care. I wanted to stop our association immediately, have her take the safe. But I felt I was already an accomplice. I was terrified that the cops would come after me, and I would end up in jail, or worse. Willie Oz was an FBI agent. Patterson, the most dangerous of the two, was also a fed. I was in it up to my neck. On the other hand, I was also outraged by what those two had done, especially Patterson, to those young women. I'll tell you the truth, I wanted to expose them, to make them pay for what they'd done."

"But what brought you to Denver?"

"Ramona called me a few days later to tell me that she'd hired a private detective, an ex-cop in Denver to find Patterson's victims. This detective hadn't tracked down any of the victims, but he'd found that a man, Jesse Latour, was the son of one of the women. Ramona tried to talk with Latour by phone. But he had shunned her, too—her words. She thought I'd stand a better chance to gain his trust—man to man, that sort of thing. By then, I had worked myself up into a rage. However, I was also sure I was sitting on a great story, one that had to be told. So I called the number she gave me, which turned out to be the coffeehouse Jesse frequents. Ramona gave me four thousand dollars, no strings attached, to pursue the story. I brought two thousand with me and the other two I left for my sister Bea to have. I was too young when my parents had Bea committed. But I always felt I should've done something to stop them. I owed my sister."

"So you came to Denver looking for Latour. How did you manage to gain his trust? Seems to me he's a tough nut to crack."

"I showed him copies of the documents in the safe, copies of the photos of the women—Patterson's victims. He recognized his mother. She died last year in Santiago. After she died, a great-aunt confessed to him the circumstances of his birth. After Felicia Latour was raped, she wouldn't consider ending the pregnancy. She was a devout Catholic. She decided to leave Denver and take refuge with some of her friends in Albuquerque. Jesse was born there. When he was a year old, Felicia decided to go back to Chile. Jesse was devastated when he learned he was Patterson's child. He wanted revenge. So he decided to come back to the States. He'd been involved with a student resistance group in Chile. One of his friends there put him in touch with someone in Chiapas, Mexico. This guy had been involved in the Zapatista movement there. Jesse spent a few months in Mexico. He was not directly involved with the Zapatistas, but the people he dealt with were. Apparently, he was asked to bring some documents and other Zapatista propaganda to sympathizing groups in Albuquerque and Denver."

"How did he manage to cross the border?" Dora asked. "I understand he applied for a Social Security number and the SSA granted it."

"Easy. He flew into Albuquerque from Mexico City. He had a Chilean passport. INS granted him a visitor's visa. He was a U.S. citizen by birth. All he had to do was to supply his birth certificate and all pertinent information to the SSA. He's very resourceful, even though he doesn't speak English that well yet. He even managed to get a driver's license, though he doesn't own a car. He got himself a job as a janitor in the warehouse across from the body shop. He works nights. I needed to support myself while I was in Denver. He knows the people at the car wash and he got me a job there. We share an apartment about a block from the coffeehouse. It makes it easier in terms of expenses and to get the information I need to write my story."

"So you're going ahead with it, no matter what. Very commendable of you."

"Don't get me wrong. I'm scared shitless. But now, it isn't just writing the story and what's in it for me, not after I've seen what all

of this did to Ramona and now to Jesse. This is personal, now. I really feel that Patterson and people like him should be publicly exposed
and brought to justice. I have to pursue this story."

"Did you or Jesse make any attempt to contact Patterson?" Dora
asked.

"We've been trying to track him down. So far, we know he's no
longer with ATF or in Denver. Do you know where we can find him?"

"We'll get to him in due time," Dora answered, trying not to
sound evasive. "Right now, we have the cops to worry about. Any
minute, the cops are going to be asking you again what you have to
do with this. I'm concerned for you. We need to go over what you're
going to tell them. So first of all, did you know Jesse had a gun and
carried it with him? Does he have a permit for it?"

"He told me he has a permit. I never asked him to produce it,
though. It's not difficult to get a gun if you have local ID. All he had
to do was wait ten working days to obtain a permit."

"I doubt Patterson knew about you two before, so why did Jesse
feel he needed that kind of protection?"

"Jesse was almost run over by a speeding car while he was crossing a street. I was waiting for him at the coffeehouse. It was about a
week after I arrived in Denver. I had already shown him copies of the
documents in the safe. After the near hit-and-run, Jesse became paranoid. I tried to convince him that Patterson couldn't have known about
him, that the driver of the car was probably on her cell phone and
didn't see him. But there was no convincing him otherwise. That's
when he got the gun. Come to think of it, does Patterson know about
Willie Oz's safe?" Vincent became very agitated.

"Patterson is no longer with ATF or in Denver; you're right about
that. I'm sure he knows nothing about Oz's safe yet. He's running for
office in the next California state elections. Who knows how far he'll
get. I had to turn in the safe and its contents to the police in Oakland."

"Shit . . . It doesn't sound good," Vincent said. He wiped the sweat
off his forehead and upper lip with his hand. "We're all in danger.
Totally."

"No kidding!" To offer some comfort, Dora added, "I doubt Patterson is going to be able to do anything to any of us at this point, not

with the police looking so closely into his affairs." She tried to sound convincing. "But look. Let's talk about your situation. I'm not a lawyer, but a word of advice: I don't think the cops have enough of a case against you. They would have booked you already. I suggest you tell them what you know. They'll probably want you as a material witness if they decide to build a case against Latour, mostly because of his association with subversive groups. Even if Jesse has a permit for the gun, he might still be charged with carrying a concealed weapon. But other circumstances factor in. For example, he really didn't know who I was. He was acting in self-defense. This whole business with Patterson makes Jesse a sympathetic figure. The only problem I see is that this kind of argument cuts both ways. If it goes to trial, the D.A. can also claim that he came back to the United States to avenge his mother. Motive. I think it's better for you to tell the cops everything you know or you might be tried as an accomplice in a conspiracy."

"I can't. I'm not being brave. I just can't betray Jesse," he said adamantly. "I'm a journalist—freelance, of course. But I have published articles in magazines and periodicals. I'm protected . . . I think. But if not, I'd rather go to jail than betray Jesse."

Dora patted Vincent on the shoulder. "Let's hope it doesn't come to any of that. Talk with Luis anyway; ask him to refer you to a good lawyer," Dora emphasized as she saw Officer Cedilla walking down the hall in their direction. Looking at his face, she could not ascertain if the news he carried was good or bad.

"Ms. Saldaña, you're free to go," Cedilla said.

"Go? Back to Oakland?"

"For now. OPD confirmed your statements regarding the case in Oakland. But the investigation here is a different matter. You'll be subpoenaed to appear if the D.A. decides to file charges against Mr. Latour. You know the penalties if you don't show up. You can pick up your belongings, gun, and license with the clerk at Evidence."

"What about Mr. Constantino? Is he free to go, too?" Dora ventured to ask.

Addressing Vincent, the officer said, "You're not being charged with anything. But you can't leave Denver. You're a material witness. Mr. Latour's arraignment is tomorrow morning, 10 o'clock. You must be present in court tomorrow. If you skip town, you'll be considered a felon. *¿Me entiendes bien?*"

Vincent acquiesced with a head nod and began to step back. Thanking the officer, who was momentarily on his way down the hall, Dora turned to Vincent.

"You're going to have to help me down the stairs. I have to pick up my gun and wallet. We need to regroup, talk with Luis. Please," she begged while she looked for a seat so she could put her sock and shoe back on.

Vincent helped her to loosely tie her shoe. She put her arm around his shoulders, and he slid his other arm around her waist to help her walk down the stairs. When they reached the evidence room, she waited outside while Dora went in to sign for her property.

When Dora joined him a while later, Vincent said, "I think you're right. It's a good idea to retain a lawyer. Will you talk with Luis about it? I need to go home right now."

"Good. I'll come with you." She thought he would object, but he seemed rather pleased at the suggestion. As they waited for a cab, she called Luis and briefed him on the events at the police department. She would call him again later.

The blizzard had begun to take force. The airport would probably be closed soon, the taxi driver told her when she inquired about it. She would probably have to wait the storm out.

Vincent and Dora arrived at his apartment only to find the cops had already been there, gathering evidence, which included every scrap of paper they had found with Jesse's name on it, as well as Vincent's tapes of interviews with Latour, his laptop and disks, and the manuscript he had been working on.

"You might want to reconsider telling the cops all you know. It might be the only way to get your stuff back," Dora said. But Vincent did not seem concerned about it, as he always made backup copies of all his files and kept the disks in a safe deposit box at the bank.

The apartment was in total disarray, and Dora suggested that Vincent spend the night in her hotel suite. He agreed.

Dora soaked her ankle in hot water, then took a long bath. By the time Luis came calling, ointment and bandage in hand, she was feeling somewhat more refreshed. Her ankle seemed to be healing, although it was still tender.

Vincent had fallen asleep on the sofa in front of the television. He woke up when he heard Luis and Dora talking. Luis had stopped by the police department to inquire about the disposition of Jesse Latour's case. Luis had been able to get one of his friends at the Public Defender's Office to represent Latour the next morning. Vincent had to be in court as well the next morning, he told her, confirming what Officer Cedilla had said.

Luis and Vincent talked for a long while. After their talk, Luis was convinced that the charges of international terrorism would not stick. The D.A. was grasping at straws. Vincent would be off the hook in that respect. Latour, however, was looking at the maximum sentence for the concealed weapon charge. Still, the scenario could change. Smelling a juicy news story, reporters were already tapping their sources at the Denver police department, Luis informed Vincent and Dora.

Dora limped after Luis to the elevator. "Thank you for everything," she said.

He smiled. She looked into his eyes, then at his mouth, slightly parted. She stretched her arm out, put her hand on his cheek, and impulsively took a step towards him. He did not move but raised his hand and stroked her hair lightly. A few strands of her hair rose on end. Her eyes closed for a second as she felt the prick of desire on the nape of her neck and shoulders. It quickly traveled down to her belly and nestled there like a swarm of bees. But her mind issued a warning. A kiss might lead to a "good morning." Was she, or Luis for that matter, ready for the aftermath? She stepped back.

Luis made no effort to come closer, perhaps because he was thinking along the same lines as she. Dora saw his disappointment flash in his eyes, then disappear behind his reserved smile. The bell announced the arrival of the elevator. He waved at her and disappeared behind the elevator doors.

When Dora got back to her room Vincent was already snoring away on the sofa. She applied ointment to her ankle and bandaged it, then got under the covers after putting one of the pillows under her leg to keep her foot raised. She turned off the light.

Sleep had been a rare commodity in the past few days. Her body ached, but not because of her injuries, and for a while she feasted on a sexual fantasy. She heard Vincent talking in his sleep. She was not grateful for the interruption, but turned her attention to what he was saying. She could not make sense of it. It was probably just a nightmare brought about by the earlier events. Vincent had good reasons to be worried.

She was not one to always ponder what the next day would bring. But with Patterson still at large and Vincent still undecided, uncertainty reigned unchallenged in her heart.

TWENTY-SIX
Desire's Demons

THE SUN WAS BEGINNING TO SHINE on a snow-blanketed Denver when Dora and Vincent woke up at seven-fifteen. Dora checked her foot and ankle. The swelling was considerably down and her sock and shoe went in, but not without some effort.

She and Vincent shared a cup of coffee, got dressed, and had breakfast at a restaurant downtown. When they finally arrived at the courthouse, Luis was waiting for them. The district attorney had decided not to pursue charges of terrorism against Latour, offering a deal instead. Latour would spend a year in jail, followed by a two-year probation for the concealed weapon charge. It was a good offer, Luis told them. But Latour was reluctant to accept the deal. He wanted his day in court. He wanted to expose Patterson, especially after he saw a short article in the paper about his case. Although his case had not made the front page, he was sure a trial would attract news-thirsty reporters.

Vincent asked Luis for some paper. He wrote a note to Jesse and asked Luis to get it to the public defender.

"I'm asking him to trust me. I'll make sure his story is known to every reporter and newspaper in town. I'll finish the book ASAP," Vincent told them as he passed the note to Luis.

Luis agreed to be the messenger and went to look for the public defender. It was almost ten o'clock when Luis returned. Latour had accepted the deal. There was nothing else to do there. Luis excused himself, as he still had some business to take care of in court. So Dora called a cab. She dropped Vincent off at his apartment on her way to her hotel.

"You don't have to stay in Denver to write your book," she said. But Vincent was determined to remain closer to Jesse and keep his promise to him.

"I'm sorry things turned out this way for Jesse," Dora said.

"It might be better for him. At least in jail he'll be safe from his father. I'll make enough noise to make sure no harm comes to Jesse."

"But what about you? If you succeed, the story is going to make headlines here and in California. You'll be mentioned by name."

"A risk I'll have to take. I'll keep a low profile, change jobs, and move."

In transit to her hotel, Dora called several airlines to check on possible flights to Oakland or San Francisco. With so many travelers stranded in Denver, she felt lucky to book a seat on an afternoon flight to Phoenix. She'd have to be on stand-by for a late evening flight from Phoenix to Oakland. If lucky, she wouldn't be home till around midnight, but at least she would be home.

"Do you think Latour accepted the deal just to keep Vincent out of jail?" Dora asked Luis when he picked her up to take her to the airport.

"It wouldn't surprise me. With Vincent in prison, who would tell or write Latour's story?"

"Sounds about right," she answered. She was quiet for a while. Luis glanced at her. She looked at him out of the corner of her eye. Her heart began to race. Music to appease desire's demons, she thought, and reached for the tuning knob. She had trouble finding a station she liked. Luis reached for the radio panel to push a button. In doing so, he brushed her arm. Myriad electric ants rushed up their respective limbs while Satchmo's voice followed the saints marching in. They both laughed.

"Not what I had in mind," Luis said.

Glances teeming with desire, electrifying caresses, and chains of unspoken words—perhaps all they had been meant to have between them. She held a sigh in. Better that way, Dora told herself, as she always did in similar situations. Coward, her mother's voice admonished within her. Her inner child ignored the remark.

"I'm heading home. You're home already," she said after a pause.

"Doesn't have to be that way," he commented, but he did not say the magic word: "Stay."

The airport terminal came into view. She unbuckled and leaned forward. She brushed his lips with hers, then quickly got out of the car. "If you ever find your way to the Bay Area, look me up."

"That's a promise."

EPILOGUE
Destiny's Designs

IT WAS ONE OF THOSE BALMY, rose-scented, late May evenings in Oakland, the kind that held a promise of fruit, longer and warmer days, and the evening fragrance of jasmine come summer.

Justin sat on the back porch with an open book in his hand. But he had stopped reading. It was nice to sit still for a moment, hear the sound of the water cascading down in the angel fountain in the garden, listen to the pleasant symphony of Gloria's clatter in the kitchen as she prepared dinner. Her mother and daughter helped with the housework. Usually he cooked, especially when there was much to celebrate. It was Gloria's birthday. He was about to ask Gloria to marry him. They were also welcoming Dora Saldaña as the third partner at Brown Angel Security and Investigations. But with his shoulder still numb and stiff, it was difficult for him to manage even shaving some mornings.

He heard the doorbell, then Dora and Beatrice's voices as they greeted everyone in the kitchen. Art Bello, Myra Miranda, Tito Figueroa and a date, Gloria's brothers and sisters-in-law, and Justin's sisters and their respective husbands would be arriving soon.

Beatrice did not take no for an answer and immediately began to set the table. Dora joined Justin in the garden. Throwing a furtive glance towards the kitchen, she handed him a small velvet case.

"Thanks for picking it up," he said, taking the case and opening it.

"No problem. It's a beautiful ring. Emerald, her birthstone, and diamonds. Gloria'll love it," she said.

"I hope so. . . ."

"What? You think she'll say no? Rest assured. I told you. When I asked her why you two hadn't gotten married already, she told me that the subject had never come up. I asked her if she would marry you. She said, and I quote, 'Absolutely.'"

A train whistled in the distance. They stopped talking and looked at each other. Neither of them would ever again be able to listen to a train whistle without thinking about the tragic events after Ramona's accident at Vista Point a month earlier. It had been the beginning of the end for Ramona M. Serna, who two weeks later had died. But Baby Gabi's life had been saved by her biological great-grandmother's bone marrow. Mrs. Serna had finally done something good for her daughter.

Serena Saucedo was in the clear with the police, but she would have to undergo a series of cosmetic operations to repair a broken cheek and nasal bone and facial scars. Although the news media had been more than kind to the Saucedos, the latter had put off their political aspirations for more auspicious times. They'd be back in the political arena soon enough, Justin and Dora were certain. They were just as sure Pretty Boy Patterson's political career was over. The statute of limitations with respect to his crimes had run out long ago. With Oz, Ramona, and Felicia dead, and his other victims in Denver unable to file charges against him, prosecution was a waste of time.

But Dora had supplied her copies of Oz's documents to the press. Patterson's face had been plastered on the front pages of every newspaper in California and Colorado. He would never be free of the shadow of suspicion. His attempts to vindicate himself publicly so far had failed. He had even received death threats after his picture was posted on the Web by rape victim watch groups. He was believed to be hiding somewhere in the Sierra Nevada Mountains.

"What do you think? Have we seen the last of Pretty Boy Patterson?" Dora asked. "I hate unfinished business."

"Difficult to predict what he might do next. But one false move on his part and he'll have the FBI all over him. He's a thorn in their side. He made the feds lose face. They'll never forgive him for that."

The doorbell rang again, announcing the arrival of the other guests. An instant later, Art Bello appeared at the door to the garden.

"News about Patterson. I just heard it on the radio. C'mon!" Art signaled for Justin and Dora to go into the house.

They walked in and found everyone in the living room watching a live report. Justin reached for Gloria's hand. Dora stood next to Justin.

A television newscaster said, "To recap for our viewers, Ron W. Patterson, former ATF agent and allegedly responsible for the rape of many women in the Bay Area and Denver, was found shot in a cabin on Echo Summit two hours ago. He was pronounced dead on arrival at Sierra Memorial Hospital. So far, the police has ruled his death a suicide. A press conference has been scheduled for eight o'clock this evening. We'll bring you live coverage of it. Right now, let's go live to our correspondent David Ortega in Denver. David, I understand you were able to speak with Jesse Latour and Vincent Constantino there."

Two small screen windows showed Jesse and Vincent. After some brief remarks about their identity and role in the story, David Ortega spoke first to Jesse in Spanish, then translated his remarks and questions to English. "Mr. Latour, I understand the police just informed you that Ron W. Patterson is dead. How do you feel about it?"

"*Me entristece sólo que mi madre y Ramona M. Serna no estén vivas para ser testigas de esto, para ver que hay justicia, aunque ésta sea sólo poética, en la vida.*" (It saddens me that my mother and Ramona M. Serna are no longer alive to witness this, to see that there is justice in life, even if it's only poetic justice.) "*Pero no me regocijo frente al cadáver, de quién fue este hombre en vida. Ve usted. Él era mi padre. Espero algún día perdonarlo por todo el mal que hizo.*" (But I don't rejoice before this man's dead body of who he was in life. You see, he was my father. I hope one day to forgive him for all the suffering he caused.)

Ortega thanked Jesse Latour and asked Vincent the same question.

"I'm not as compassionate and forgiving a man as Jesse Latour. I truly believe Patterson was an evil man. I never thought I would say this and mean it. The world is a much better place without Pretty Boy Patterson in it. He abused his power as an agent for the government. Saddest of all, he, like many others, was sanctioned to abuse his power by the very government agencies that are supposed to protect those who can't protect themselves."

Jesse Latour had granted Ortega exclusive interviews through interpreters and had agreed to appear in Spanish-speaking talk shows upon his release from prison. His interviews were scheduled to air closer to the time Vincent Constantino's book, *Fate's Victims*, would see first light. Many hailed Jesse as a hero, in particular for his efforts on behalf of the Zapatista movement in Chiapas. Vincent was negotiating the sale of his manuscript for an undisclosed six-figure royalty advance. He had plans to share the proceeds with Jesse Latour and his sister, who lived in Oakland, California. With the help of the Saucedo family in Oakland, he hoped to establish the Ramona María Serna Literary Prize for underrepresented Latina writers in Colorado and California.

"The feds sure know how to pull their thorns out," Dora told Justin. She sighed.

"They sure do." He raised an eyebrow and smiled sadly.

With Patterson's death, some sense of justice and order had been restored. But not all was well, Dora knew. Not with Justin. That evening by the train tracks, he had fired the shot that had taken William Ozuna's life. One day, she prayed, her new friend and partner would stop waking up in the dead of night, his heart pounding in his chest like a caged bird yearning for unbound flight. One day, she prayed, her new friend and partner would stop waking up in the dead of night, his heart pounding in his chest like a caged bird yearning for unbound flight.